# THE ADVENTURES OF
# GEORGE LEE

*May 17, 2017*

# ORVILLE MANN

*To Joyce w/ Love*

*Orville Mann*

# THE ADVENTURES OF
# GEORGE LEE

## A RACE AGAINST TIME

## TATE PUBLISHING
### AND ENTERPRISES, LLC

Published by Tate Publishing & Enterprises, LLC
127 E. Trade Center Terrace | Mustang, Oklahoma 73064 USA
1.888.361.9473 | www.tatepublishing.com

Tate Publishing is committed to excellence in the publishing industry. The company reflects the philosophy established by the founders, based on Psalm 68:11,
*"The Lord gave the word and great was the company of those who published it."*

Published in the United States of America

ISBN: 978-1-68333-070-7
Fiction / Thrillers / Military
16.04.01

## Rewarded Efforts

After returning from a week of reconnaissance, 1st Lieutenant George Edward Lee was now back in his quarters, preparing to report to the commander's office. As he was getting ready for breakfast, something reminded him of how different life for him today is than it was during his childhood back on the Indiana farm of his childhood.

In his youth, he had been quiet and extremely shy.

He thought, *Perhaps people would say I was more than slightly introverted.*

That reminded him of a psychological test he took during his twenties. It revealed that he had traits of an ambivert. An ambivert, according to the definition he received, is someone who has characteristics of both an introvert and an extravert. The term defines a person who is willing to aid someone in need and yet when placed in a leadership position shows initiative and has the capability of resolutely addressing situations as they confront him.

Be that as it may, while in high school, his introvertive side generally prevailed. A handsome young man, he attracted some girls who were interested in becoming friendlier, but because of his shyness, he struggled to respond to any effort to have a conversation. He simply would blush and turn away when he noticed a young lady smiling at him.

His grandparents reared George on the family farm, but because they were very poor, they were afforded none of the finer things of life. However, in one thing they were quite rich; in their love for George. They demonstrated and lavished upon him every bit of the love they possibly could. They began showing that love shortly after his birth when they took him into their home to rear as their own child. Initially, his birth parents left him with the grandparents because of their inability to properly care for their baby, which was weak and ill. Also, they could not afford the extra medical expense. They visited quite often and always kept in touch with George so that he knew that they loved him. His siblings would sometimes visit the farm for weeks at a time. Those were times of getting to know them as family.

George's work ethic was taught through example by his grandparents. When he was in his early teens, he worked side by side with his grandfather cutting corn before the sun's heat evaporated the morning dew. They used corn knives similar in design to a machete, except that the end is much broader which is quite blunt. The reason they would start the harvest early in the mornings was that the corn leaves were still flexible and did not scratch the skin as much as when they were dry. After cutting the corn in the moonlight, they cut and stacked several stalks together and tie them into bundles called "shocks." The shocks were up to three feet in diameter and tied with binder twine or a stalk of corn, then stood up on end until the time for shucking. When the sun started to dry out the corn, they would stop work and go to the house where George's grandmother would have a warm delicious breakfast waiting for them.

After a few weeks, the seeds hardened into kernels. When the whole crop was ready, the shocks were laid on the ground and untied. The ears of corn were removed from the stalk, shucked, husked, and the silk was removed. The corn was laid on a burlap (gunny) sack until they had piles enough for a wagon load. Then the shucked corn was hauled to the crib for storage until it was sold or used to feed the chickens or livestock.

Sure, farming was hard work, but there were many exciting benefits, or at least George thought so. From early youth, he had quite a variety of animals to care for and sometimes play with. He had several loving pets, but there were a few unfriendly residents that passed through the barnyard, hog pens, and chicken houses.

One such unfriendly creature was Billy, the patriarch of the goat clan. Billy's color was medium brown with dark brown streaks bordered in white. The stripes started between his horns and extend down his back to the tip of his tail. He strutted around the barnyard like it was his personal domain. He had a goatee and two one-inch long dangling growths under and behind his lower jaws, one tang dangled on each side of the chin. His big horns curled upward and backward from just above his eyes and curved back under and outward until they pointed forward. They looked similar to big horned sheep's horns.

If you were not the target of a solid butt, you would probably think that he was a beautiful animal. But through much experience, he had learned how to use his horns to successfully bully the smaller and weaker female goats and, at times, George, if he happened to be on his turf. Billy assumed the position as head of the clan and defended that position with routine patrols.

Besides his dislike for George, Billy had another distinct and equally distasteful characteristic. He gave off a peculiar and sometimes terrible smelling odor, especially when he was angry or interested in one of his harem. It seemed that Billy's foul smell intensified any time that George was near.

The singular nicest thing George remembered about Billy was that he sired beautiful kids that often became his pets. He loved to watch the kids frolic and playfully butt heads or perhaps climb to the top of the barnyard gate. The gate was made of 3/4 inches thick boards, but the kids had no trouble walking across the very top slat of the gate. A goat's climbing ability never ceased to intrigue George.

He felt a responsibility to learn how to communicate with the goats, so he tried to learn a variety of goat bleats and their meanings. George smiled as he recalled how the twenty or so goats would come stampeding toward him from all across the pasture in response to his bleating call (bah-ma-ah).

George mimicked the sounds of other farm animals he helped care for, from the moo of a large cow to the cheeps of small chickens. He became so proficient that, to his amazement, one evening, he was successful in calling a wild whippoorwill to within a couple feet of where he was standing in the shadow of a tree on a moonlit night. He had laughed at the bird's reaction when it realized that a human being, and not a potential mate, had called him that night. It hastily fluttered away, very disappointed, George surmised.

George thought it amusing to have an animal respond to his call and look for one of their kind. Cats would have trouble finding the unseen cat that mewed when George was around. Dogs would run to the door when he barked, expecting to find a dog behind the door. Outside, the dogs would turn toward the lane expecting to see a vehicle coming down the driveway.

George had very little success in becoming friends with chickens, ducks, geese, and guineas, but occasionally had success with a pigeon.

A local distillery supplied mash, which worked really well when it was feeding time or time to "slop" the hogs. The mesh, the leftovers from the liquor brewing process, was not supposed to be fermented, but for some reason, the hogs really loved it.

Some of the animals, in addition to the harvested crops and garden vegetables, provided plenty of food for the family. Cabbage and apples were stored for winter consumption in holes dug in the ground and encompassed with fallen leaves or straw which acted as insulation; the provisions were laid on a bed of leaves or straw and then covered with the same. Then the food with its insulation was covered with a thick layer of earth. During the winter, when food was needed from the stash, a family member would simply dig into the mound—sometimes snow covered—and remove the desired amount. They would restore the insulation of leaves or straw and cover it over again with soil. These provisions along with canned peaches and tomatoes and staples like cornbread or biscuits and beans kept the family well fed during the winter months.

George's childhood, playing with the animals and learning about rabbits, opossums, raccoons, squirrels, and foxes, was a happy one. Anxious moments occurred when he would have a surprise meeting on occasion with an equally surprised snake. The time that he was gathering kindling for the cookstove was a typical example of such an occasion. Bark from a fallen beech tree quickly started fires in the cooking range. The log he chose was about three feet, six inches in diameter with bark remaining on the log but peeling away because the log had lain out in the weather and sun for several years. As he pulled the loosening bark away, a large black snake fell to the ground at his bare feet. George jumped and took off like a greased pig at the county fair when all the kids were after it. He left his chore with his newly found serpent friend. Try as he might, he could not remember if the bark was ever retrieved for lighting fires in Mom's kitchen stove.

During his early teens, George had an additional experience with slithering creature-friends. On one such occasion, he was plowing a field that was to be planted in corn. On one of the rounds around the field a movement caught his attention. He quickly turned toward the movement and saw that he had uncovered a nest of snakes during the previous plowing round. Several snakes from the nest had wrapped themselves around the wheel in the furrow. They were writhing and squirming, flicking out their forked tongues at the top of the wheel near to George's seat. Frightened nearly to death by what he saw next to him, he pressed in the clutch, kicked the gearshift into neutral, and abandoned the tractor with the engine still running.

Of course, he jumped off the opposite side from where the snakes were dangling. He ran to find his grandfather.

"Grandpa, you will have to go get the tractor, I just ran over a nest of snakes. I left the tractor engine running there in the field."

His grandpa laughed as George explained what had happened. He was kind enough to go and get the tractor, but he never mentioned if the snakes were gone when he got to the tractor. Perhaps these occasions are a part of the reason that he had near nightmares about snakes being wrapped around his body, which, as he fell over a cliff, stared into his eyes as they flicked out forked tongues. Thankfully for him, even though his heart was pounding, he always awakened just before he and his companions struck the ground.

George's parents were converted to the Christian faith, and soon afterward, his father felt a call into the ministry. He held revivals and he and George's mother would sing. He also pastored several churches in Southern Indiana, Kentucky, and Ohio. They continued their ministry until he retired during their early '70s to a small ranch in Iowa.

When George pondered his childhood incidents, he had warm feelings. Even the snake dreams would be better than listening to today's evening news. The human treatment of others, murders, tortures, child abuses, and many other disturbing items were distressing. Such things never ceased to amaze and sometimes depress him.

Now concentrating on the present, he prayed, "Oh, God, what is our world coming to? What has happened to humanity in our supposedly civilized world? Please, God, help me to be instrumental in making this world a better place where God's love will be accepted in the hearts of our multitudes of people."

$$\longrightarrow\!\!\!\!\!\!\!\bullet\!\!(\!(\!|\!)\!)\!\!\bullet\!\!\!\!\!\!\!\longrightarrow$$

As George looked in the mirror and straightened his coal-black hair and adjusted his tie, he saw a six-foot, medium-built, and deeply tanned man wearing an army dress uniform with several service ribbons pinned on his left lapel. He decided that he looked presentable enough for the day and turned toward the kitchen to prepare and eat breakfast.

After breakfast, he walked down to the street to where Sergeant Harry Collins, his assigned driver for the past year, waited by a military staff car. Lieutenants usually are not chauffeured around in staff cars, but because the importance of his special assignment, the commanding officer had ordered it. Collins snapped to attention and saluted as George approached and, of course, the lieutenant returned the salute before he got into the backseat.

Sergeant Collins was a somewhat stocky man with a pleasant smile and strong build. His light brown burr haircut appeared almost red next to his slight tan. As they pulled away, he looked in the rearview mirror and greeted

George, "Hello, Lieutenant Lee, how are you doing this beautiful morning, sir? I hope you had a pleasant flight back from your assignment."

As they turned left on Broadway, George answered, "I'm fine. And yes, the flight was very pleasant and the meetings and recon were rewarding and beneficial. How are you doing, Sergeant Collins?"

Collins answered, "I'm pretty tired. Pam and I had a rough night because the baby kept us up complaining of a stomachache."

George recalled Pamela's looks. She was a bit shorter than Harry, probably five feet tall, with long black hair that hung to her waist. She had a reddish complexion, likely because of her American Indian heritage, which was part Navajo if George remembered correctly.

"That's too bad, Harry, children sometimes do that. How old is Tommy now? Almost two, I'd guess," George responded.

"Sir, you have a good memory," Harry commented.

George was grateful. "Thanks, Sergeant, I hope Tommy gets better before we are sent on the upcoming assignment. Harry, do you have any idea of what's on my agenda for today?"

Harry looked serious. "Let me remind you that you have a meeting with the CO this morning at 1000 hours. He sounded serious when he talked with me about it yesterday."

After arriving at the office, George completed his report. He made recommendations concerning his reconnoiter of a remote Pacific island that was formerly used by the military as a refuel stop when their flights were routed near the island. He had gone there to check it out as a potential research and development site. The newly formed unit would be working there if his recommendation were approved by the upper echelon. About 0930 hours, he headed into the latrine to check out his appearance and then headed to meet with the CO of Headquarters and Headquarters Company.

He knocked on the captain's door and entered, approached the desk and saluted, "Lt. Lee reporting as ordered, Captain Rankin."

Captain Larry Rankin, a tall, slightly balding, seasoned veteran, returned the salute and said with a deep baritone voice, "Good morning, Lt. Lee. Have a seat, George. How did everything go?"

George responded as he seated himself to the left of the captain's desk, "It went very well, sir, and I think the location will work well for what we have in mind. The ground covering will work as designed, and the facility should hold any heavy equipment we require. I believe it has great potential for concealing our operation. Here is a copy of my final report and recommendation."

The captain's face lit up with a bright smile as he received the report.

"That's great, Lieutenant. To change the subject a bit, I have some good news for you, George." He picked up some papers from his desk and handed them to George. "I received your orders while you were away. Congratulations. You have been promoted to the rank of captain."

George was stunned, and it took a second to soak in. "Really?"

The captain stood and walked over to George with extended hand and said, "It surely is, and congratulations once again."

George stood to receive the congratulatory handshake as Captain Rankin gave George a hug and a pat on the back. "You have been assigned the formidable task of forming and, if need be, training this new unit. However, they want you to be fresh when you begin the job, so they want you to take a couple weeks leave and spend some time with your family before you begin the assignment. Are there any questions?"

George answered, "Captain Rankin, I want you to know that it has been a great pleasure to serve under your command. I do not have any questions, but I do have a request, if I may make one?"

The CO responded, "Sure, George. What is it?"

George replied, "Well, Captain Rankin, you know that Sergeant Collins has been with me since long before I took the position here at Headquarters and Headquarters Company. Because of his skills and our ability to work well together, I would greatly appreciate it if you would arrange to promote him to the rank of first sergeant assigned to my unit, sir."

The CO walked over to a file cabinet, opened the top drawer, and retrieved Sergeant Collins's records.

After a short examination, he looked up at George, smiled, and said, "After looking at his record, I think that can be arranged, Captain Lee. Sgt. Collins has an exemplary record, and you and he seem to work well together. Thanks for the report, Lieutenant…I mean, Captain Lee. Would you like to accompany me to the mess hall for some lunch?"

George smiled and agreed as they turned toward the door. It was a pleasant lunch with light conversation, interrupted by an occasional greeting and congratulations on his promotion by the company staff.

"It seems that almost everyone knew about my promotion. I guess good news travels fast, huh, Captain Rankin?"

"I think our first sergeant must have seen the orders and spread the good news, George," the captain responded.

George asked, "Will we know about Sergeant Collins soon, sir?"

"Oh, I think it's a sure thing. We should have the approval before you take your leave this weekend, George," the captain answered.

"That is great, sir. I will let him know as soon as I get the news," Captain Rankin told George. "Better yet, you can tell him. Just a reminder, make sure you have those captain bars on your uniform before you leave here today. I think the supply room has a couple sets. After that, you can buy all you need at the PX."

George responded, "Yes, sir. I will, Captain. And thanks for allowing me to have lunch with you. May I be excused? I really need to do some things before I go on leave."

The captain stood and they shook hands and Rankin congratulated George once more as he left.

When Sergeant Collins reported to take George back to his BOQ (bachelor officer's quarters), he smiled when he saw the captain's bars.

"Wow, sir, congratulations. I'm not really that surprised though because you are a good officer and I heard the scuttlebutt at HQ."

"Harry, you are a rascal, but thank you very kindly," George responded with a grin.

The sergeant returned the smile and shook his hand and said again, "Congratulations, you deserve it, sir."

George smiled and asked, "Harry, would you consider being my first sergeant in the newly formed unit?"

"I think it would be an honor to serve under your command. Does that mean I would get a promotion too, sir, Captain?" Harry asked. "My wife will be thrilled at the news if it's true."

"Congratulations," George said, but then warned, "please don't spread this around until it's made official. The CO assured me that there would be no problem with it going through, but that it would probably be best not to tell anyone except Pam until it's confirmed."

"Sure thing, Captain. I understand," Harry responded. There was happy silence on the way to George's BOQ as both men contemplated their recent and soon-to-occur promotions.

———◉———

After dropping off Captain Lee, the soon-to-be First Sergeant Harry Collins hurried home. His wife, Pamela, met him at the door and gave him a big hug and kiss.

Harry asked, "How did your day go? And how is Tommy?"

Pam answered, "I think he is doing better. His fever has dropped down to normal. Tell me about your day, honey?"

Harry got a sheepish look as an impish smile formed. "Guess what happened on the way home?" But he could not wait for her guess and blurted out, "I'm being promoted to first sergeant."

Pam was like a young child when she got the news. She giggled and jumped up and down with glee. She gave Harry a big hug, her dark eyes aglow. "Oh, honey, that's wonderful."

Harry added, "And Lt. Lee is now Captain Lee. After the CO told him that he was to form and train the unit, he requested that I be assigned to the newly designated unit as his first sergeant. He asked me not to tell anyone but you about it before it is made official, so please, honey, do not tell anyone about this until it happens."

Pam answered, "I'm so excited. Now we can afford to buy that new crib for Tommy. So a new unit is being formed. What kind of unit is it?"

A blank look formed on Harry's face before he answered, "Pam, I'm sworn to secrecy, so I can't discuss it with anyone, including you. In fact, only a few of the upper echelon officers know that it is being formed, much less what the unit is about. I'm sure that after it gets underway, news will be released, but for now, it's top secret and nothing is being revealed about it. Captain Lee will be in charge of forming and overseeing the serious work on the top-secret assignment after he takes a couple weeks' leave. I certainly believe that he is the man for the job. Why, he even remembered Tommy's age this morning."

As they continued to talk, Harry began to get excited too. "Hey, here's an idea. Let's get Tommy dressed and you get dolled up and we will go out and celebrate."

As Harry and Pam happily readied to go out on the town, Captain Lee was making arrangements to go home for a few days.

———— ⊷«(◉)»⊶ ————

The first thing George did in planning for the trip back home was to give his parents a heads-up that he was headed their way.

When his father answered his phone call, George said, "Hello, Dad, this is George. How are you doing?" The conversation was light for a few minutes then George told him the news, "I'll be headed home this next weekend."

Mom must have heard and picked up an extension. She practically screamed, "George, honey, is it true? Are you really coming home this weekend? That is great news, son, and we will be so glad to see you. Now, you have a safe trip home. We have been praying that we would see you soon. I love you. Bye, son." George heard his mother saying as she hung up the phone, "Thank you, Jesus!"

George was happy to have heard the voices of his parents. The conversation with them brought memories of his childhood pouring back once again. He thought of riding bareback on Beauty, a black workhorse at the family farm. One thing he had to watch was that when Beauty headed for the barn. She seemed to go into racing mode, and he would sometimes lose his seating on the sharp turns. Once or twice, he almost fell off. Had he not been clinging to her long mane for dear life, he most surely would have fallen. Beauty, like Billy the goat, had a mean streak. When George was harnessing the team to do some farm chores, Beauty would try to bite him on the shoulder when the opportunity offered itself. Perhaps his reactions made matters worse. He would duck down from the bite and swing his elbow upward into her nose. Once the animosity had begun, there seemed to be no resolution to it. For some strange reason, Beauty acted with loyalty in every other situation.

Unlike Beauty, Maude, the other team horse, was always gentle and never caused any problems for George. Maude and Beauty worked well together and were able to pull tremendous loads. Lots of farm crops were harvested utilizing this team. Both of the farm horses were gone now after years of faithful service.

"Wrong thought," George said aloud. Tractors had replaced the team. Horses were nice, and it was sad to see them go, but tractors could get most things done more quickly than horses.

On the day of his departure home, Sergeant Collins took George to the airport. Pam decided to take the opportunity to go shopping in the city after they had dropped George off at the airfield. So Harry arrived with Pam and Tommy to pick up George the day of his flight. George, dressed in civvies (civilian clothing), stowed his luggage in the trunk of Harry's POV (privately owned vehicle) and insisted on allowing Pam to continue sitting in the front seat while he sat in the back with Tommy. By the time they traveled the fifty miles to the terminal, two-year-old Tommy and he were playing together like old friends. George said good-bye to Tommy and thanked Harry and Pam for the ride. He gave Harry a fifty-dollar bill.

"Now, you take your beautiful family out to lunch on me."

Harry was flabbergasted, and tears welled up in Pam's eyes.

"Thank you, Captain George. This is the second great surprise I have had this week. Have a wonderful time with your parents. Maybe someday, I will get to meet them."

George thanked them once again for the ride and told Harry and Pam to go ahead and leave him because they did not need to wait with him. "Enjoy your day together, Harry. Please do not forget to pick me up when I return. I will give you a call and let you know when."

Harry wished George a safe flight and assured him that he would pick him up upon his return.

George entered the terminal and headed for the airline's boarding section. Security checked him through without a problem. He waited for about forty-five minutes before they announced that his plane was ready for boarding. The boarding process was somewhat slow, but George had something to read and that helped him remain patient until he entered the plane and took his assigned seat. The 707 jetliner had surprisingly comfortable seats, so he hoped to get some sleep during the flight home.

All in all, the flight was smooth except for minor turbulence over the Rocky Mountains. As George looked down from the plane, he thanked God for creating such a beautiful world. Below were tiny mountain lakes and cabins that looked smaller than specks. He identified them as cabins because of the clouds of smoke rising from their chimneys. He finally began to relax as he left the responsibilities of the post behind. After about three hours, the fasten-seatbelt light came on and the pilot announced that they were making their approach for landing and that he expected to land in approximately ten minutes. As they taxied toward the terminal, the pilot thanked them for flying Conway Airlines. Then he wished them an enjoyable stay in Sioux City.

<hr />

George made his way to the baggage carousel and waited until his bags came to within reach. He verified that the baggage was his and retrieved them. Charlene, his sister, greeted him with a hug.

He asked, "Where are Mom and Pop?"

Charlene answered, "The trip would have tired them too much, and so they asked me to come, and I happily agreed. It's so great to see you, and you look well."

George put in, "Sis, you look as beautiful as ever. Tell me, do you have a serious relation with that boyfriend yet?"

She replied, "Al and I had a fight a couple weeks ago and I broke it off. I found out that he was not really a Christian. He was just putting on a show so that I would keep going out with him. Just think, I was considering marrying him. Well, let's get out of here and head to the farm."

George followed her, and as they approached the car, he remarked, "My, but someone is getting up in the world. That is a really nice vehicle, Charlene. How long have you had this?"

She answered, "A couple days. I really like it though. It drives like a dream and gets good gas mileage considering the power it has. Hop in. On second thought, do you want to drive?"

"No thanks, I have gotten used to being chauffeured on the base, so you can drive, and I will try to sit back and enjoy the ride," he replied.

<hr />

Mom and Dad were sitting on the porch awaiting their arrival. They jumped to their feet when Charlene turned her Cadillac convertible onto the lane. By the time they pulled up to the house, Mom and Dad were waiting in the yard. They rushed over and welcomed George with a handshake and a hug from Dad and a hug and kiss from Mom.

Dad told George, "Son, you look good. The army must be good for you. Mom got the news that you have been promoted to the rank of captain. Congratulations, son."

Charlene added, "Congrats from me too, George. Talk about me getting up in the world. Captain Lee! Wow!"

Dad chimed in, "Does this mean Mom and me can borrow some money to fix up the house now?"

They all had a good laugh as George grabbed his bag from the backseat and they headed inside.

"Man, it's really good to see you guys and seeing Charlene, that's a special treat," George commented.

With that special gleam in her eye, Mom said, "Supper's already on the table. I fixed everything just the way you like it. I can't believe it. You are really home. After supper, we will go out to the barn and take a look at all the new babies. You can see the new litter of pigs old Sally had the other day. We got a new colt out there too."

"Bossy had twins," Dad said.

"I have been pretty busy just caring for all the new babies," Mom added.

Supper was good, and just like Mom had said, she had all the nice things that George liked to eat as he grew up during the times he visited them during his youth. He bragged about what a good cook his mom was.

"Mom, this is some really great grub. If I were home, I would weigh 240 pounds in no time."

Charlene laughed. "Are you saying you don't weigh that much already?"

"Thank you, sis."

George tried to look hurt, but knew that she was just being her normal self. Mom looked happy with the compliments from her son. The conversation remained light until Dad asked what he was doing for the army. George tried to ignore the question until everyone at the table joined the quiz.

"Hey, you guys, I'm sorry, but I am not allowed to discuss my job with anyone. I can't even tell you where I will be working. It is top secret and I just cannot talk to anyone or tell you anything at all about it."

That seemed to satisfy everyone, for which George was grateful.

George slept well, the best night's sleep he had had in weeks. He came down to breakfast after a nice shower.

He asked, "What smells so good?"

Mom smiled and rushed over to give him a hug. "My! Son, you sure look rested this morning."

The family agreed as he entered the dining room.

They were out making sure that all the new babies were okay. Dad and he had just closed the barn door when a helicopter circled above the house and landed in the pasture close to the barn.

Dad looked at George and asked, "What in the world is going on, son?"

He answered, "I'm not sure, but I guess we will soon find out."

An army officer approached George and saluted, "Sir, I'm Lieutenant Shimura. Are you Captain Lee, sir?"

George returned the salute despite the fact that he was in work clothes. "Yes, Lieutenant. What's going on?"

As the lieutenant reached into his jacket and retrieved some papers, he responded, "I'm not quite sure, sir, but I have been sent to bring you these papers and take you back to the division headquarters ASAP, sir."

George examined the papers and told Lt. Shimura, "I will get my things and be back in a jiffy. I don't have my uniform with me."

"Sir, please wait, I'll be right back," the lieutenant replied. He ran over to the chopper and returned with the captain's uniform. "First Sgt. Collins got these from your BOQ, sir. He thought you would want them."

"Thanks, Lieutenant, I will be right back," George said, smiling. Dad followed him toward the house. George yelled for Mom and Charlene as Dad and he entered the house. "I am so sorry, but I am needed back at the base. Please forgive me, but I must leave immediately," he told them. He left them as they looked at each other in disbelief. It took him only a few moments to change into his military uniform and throw his other clothing into bags.

With tears welling up in her eyes, Mom asked, "But you have only been here overnight. Do you really need to leave right now?"

"Dad, Mom, and Charlene, it must be super important for me to have been called back. They would not have sent a helicopter after me unless it was necessary. I am really sorry, but I really must go with them. I love you three. I'm sorry, but I must go."

They exchanged hugs and kisses with him as he left the house.

Mom had tears in her eyes as she watched George hurriedly get aboard the Black Hawk. He waved as it lifted skyward, tilted to the left, and headed toward the southwest.

As it disappeared into the distance, Dad said, "He really was serious last night when he told us that he could not talk about his job. This morning's surprise helicopter visit certainly convinced me of that, how about you, Mom?"

Mom answered, "I always knew that boy would amount to something and I'm so proud of our boy."

"I guess my big brother is doing quite well for himself," Charlene put in.

## The Challenge

The helicopter flight back to the base was uneventful. As they landed on the heliport, George was happy to see First Sergeant Collins approaching the chopper. Harry smiled as they exchanged salutes and then took the captain's bags. George followed Harry to the vehicle.

"How was your flight, sir?"

George responded, "It was a good flight, Harry. How is Tommy doing?"

"He is doing great. It seemed that it was nothing more than the sniffles. Pam and I have caught up on our rest again," Harry said.

After heading back to headquarters, George asked, "What is happening Harry?"

"I'm not quite sure, but it seems that President Whinton wants this project initiated ASAP, sir," Harry replied.

It took only a short time to get to the HQ. As they headed toward the entrance, George commented, "Oh, by the way, congratulations on your promotion, First Sergeant Collins."

Harry, with a broad smile, answered, "Why, thank you, sir. And thanks for making it happen. You know that I'm grateful to you."

George looked at Harry and said, "I felt that you were most qualified to fill that position."

"Thanks for the confidence you showed in me, sir, I will try not to let you down," Harry said.

They entered HQ and everyone turned to stare at them.

George whispered, "Why is everyone staring at us?"

"I'm sure we will find out in short order, sir," Harry quietly answered as they approached the CO's office. George knocked and Harry and he entered, "Captain George Lee reporting as ordered, sir."

"Pull up a couple seats, gentlemen. I'm Colonel John Murphy, and I will be in charge of the research and development part of this program. And if things go as planned, we may assemble the weapon after it is completed. As you know it is imperative that we find an adequate defense against a newly developed and superior weapon system that has the capability of destroying a whole block with just one blast. It will be your duty to lead the newly formed company to find the means, design, and assemble the equipment necessary to destroy this menace. You will have at your disposal the necessary tools to fulfill your mission. At this moment, there is a transport waiting to take you and the sergeant to the island that you recommended. Gentlemen, I wish you both the best of luck on this critical mission."

George and Harry stood, saluted, sharply did about-faces, and left the room. As they entered the next room, one of the soldiers called the others to attention, and everyone in the room saluted the captain.

The man spoke up, "Our very existence may depend on your success, sir. We trust that God will bless you in your efforts."

The captain returned their salutes and said, "He will, I'm sure of that. Through the power of your prayers for Colonel Murphy and us, ladies and gentlemen, we will succeed. We will certainly need them if we are to succeed."

In unison, the whole room full of military personnel agreed that they would be in their prayers. George and Harry left division headquarters and headed for the airfield. On the way there, George asked Harry, "Have you informed your wife that you will be gone for a while?"

He replied, "Yes, sir. She knows I will be gone as long as it takes. Although she does not know what it is, she knows that our job is important, and I will be gone until it is done."

# Day 1

They arrived at the island located somewhere in the Pacific that George selected as the location for the project's work site. He had chosen it because he knew it had been successfully used previously for similar work and because of the security it provided. Also, the camouflage made the facility invisible from the air. The pilot radioed the tower of their approach, and as they neared the site, the runway appeared as the camouflage rolled aside. The plane landed and was quickly moved into a heavily camouflaged hangar as the runway was immediately covered by plant life once again. It was completely hidden from the air. Even if someone walked across the area, it was hidden so well that they would not suspect that under their feet, there was a concrete runway capable of receiving most military planes.

George informed Harry as they approached the field, "Only a few within the military know about this airstrip, and they are sworn to absolute secrecy. Someone found to betray its location would experience dire consequences, perhaps even death, at the President Whinton's discretion. Verification of that fact was proven in that a short while after I was picked up by the helicopter at the family farm, CIA agents drove up to the house and questioned my family about whether they had been told anything about the project we would be working on. Of course, the only thing they could report was that I had told them that I could not discuss anything about this assignment or its location.

After about three hours of conversation, the agents were satisfied that nothing had been revealed, so they thanked my family for their time and left."

Captain Lee took time to settle in and then meet with the squad leaders and the civilian scientists. Some of them were section chiefs and or department heads that had arrived a week before to familiarize themselves with the highly guarded facility and begin setting up the project. The transport took off soon after Harry, George, and the soldiers that had filled its seats had deplaned and gone into the facility. The plane had been on the ground approximately twenty minutes. George felt the heavy load of responsibility to design and build the piece of equipment the teams would utilize to deter the success of one of the world's most active aggressors.

Thankfully, the government had hired a couple of mechanical engineers in addition to the group of scientists. Before they went to their quarters, George instructed Harry to have the troop's formation at 0700 hours the next morning.

Hopefully, if they were successful, the defensive weapon would be capable of stopping the enemy's weapon from firing its destructive beam. The weapon must not be allowed to fire one single bombardment beam. It must be destroyed first.

# Day 2

Harry called the formation to attention as Captain Lee's entrance.

George addressed the troops, "At ease."

The sound of the troops moving their left legs to the at-ease position resounded in the auditorium. He continued, "I wanted to take this opportunity to meet with you and introduce myself before we become so involved with our work that we no longer have the time for such formalities. Good morning, ladies and gentlemen, I'm Captain George Lee, the commanding officer to the military personnel and CEO to you civilians. Most of you have already met Lt. Dewitt and First Sergeant Collins, who will have charge of the military personnel. First Lieutenant Patrick Dewitt will serve as head of the security. Along with some others, he and his platoon have been here for a week setting up the security equipment and studying the layout of the facility and grounds. I have just met Lt. Dewitt, but Sergeant Collins and I have served together for several months and during a couple tours of combat duty. He has battle experience and is a very capable soldier and is not one to be messed with. I would not advise anyone to do that, verbally or physically.

"Ladies and gentlemen, you have all been selected because you possess some applicable skill or training that will be of value to our mission. Our mission is top secret, and you will receive information on a-need-to-know basis. This location will remain isolated from everything off this island. There will be no contact with anyone outside this island except through me. There will be weekly mail deliveries at which time you can send letters to you family. No calls will be made except by me and those will be primarily to contact HQ as necessary in relation to our mission. Only in case of emergency will anyone be allowed to leave until the mission is completed. There will be absolutely no smoking allowed inside the facility because of the possibility of fire. There will be no smoking outside because of the possibility of being seen by satellite. Anyone caught smoking will suffer dishonorable discharge and court-martials. No one is allowed outside at night except on special assignments. We must not chance discovery of the fact that we are here. There are satellites above us that could possibly find our location and alert the prying eyes of our enemies. Therefore, it is imperative that we make every possible effort to keep our work here a secret. I say once again, this is a top priority, top secret, and very sensitive project. We must not be found. Be aware that if there are any security leaks, the perpetrator can expect to spend the next few decades in some obscure location, perhaps near the North Pole. And consider this, the penalty, at the discretion of the president, may be death. A serious breach of security certainly will result in the death penalty. We certainly do not want that to happen. Do we? Well, do we?"

Captain Lee waited for their response.

"No, sir," they all responded in unison.

He continued, "All right! Ladies and gentlemen, during our stay here, we will be under close scrutiny. On the lighter side, you will have all the exercise, food, and down time that you need. We will enjoy privileges that are offered to very few other units in the US Army. You will be expected to perform at your best while on duty and work diligently toward the goal of finding some means to accomplish your group's assignment. I am not exaggerating when I tell you that this is one of the most critical missions you have ever been a part of. Remember this! Your life and the life of your families may depend on the successful completion of our mission here. Are we on the same page with this?"

As a unit, everyone including the civilian workers responded, "Yes, sir."

"Can we get this done?"

"Yes, sir."

"One more thing, if you get any ideas that you think may be beneficial to the success of this mission, please write it down and give it to an NCO, officer, or your team leader. Thank you. Does anyone have a question?"

"No, sir," the formation answered in unison.

George finished with "Thanks for your efforts and God's speed." He then directed an ordered to Harry, "First Sergeant, post."

First Sergeant Collins moved to the head of the formation and saluted.

"Take charge of the company," Captain Lee ordered.

Sergeant Collins saluted smartly. "Yes, sir."

He did an about-face and addressed the troops, "Company, attention."

As Captain Lee marched to the door, he heard Sergeant Collins give the order, "Squad leaders, move your squads out to their respective duties."

## Day 3

The next day, George visited the various departments in the facility and checked out security. The scientists were working with the soldiers assigned to their respective sections. George took note of the concerted effort being made to identify the method used to create such destructive force the new weapon was believed to be capable of. The only item they had to confirm that it existed and had such destructive power were satellite images taken from several miles above earth's atmosphere. The CIA had tried to discover its power source, but their agents either returned unsuccessful or went missing when they went searching for it. George believed that his soldiers and the scientists working as teams were to expedite development of a means to destroy the enemy's new weapon.

The engineers began drafting blueprints for the new equipment so George dropped by the laboratory of Dr. Charles Piton, the lead scientist who was leading a discussion about the satellite photos of the test firing of the enemy's weapon and the possible chemical composition the blast colors represented. What chemical combination could create such force? He turned and faced George as he entered the room.

"Good morning, Captain Lee. How are you doing this morning, sir?"

George gave the typical response. "I'm doing quite well. And how are you?"

"I'm doing fine, thank you. I think we have some good news to report. My team of scientists and I believe that we may have discovered a breakthrough. An examination of the enhanced photo reveals unusual chemical compositions. The next step will be to duplicate the same mixture when we activate our own weapon. Once that is accomplished, we can begin work on a means of effective destruction of the enemy's latest weapon. I have already instructed the team to begin designing a small version of the weapon. We should have one ready within four to five weeks. I thank God for the good team that I have working with me, Captain."

"Dr. Piton, that is certainly is good news. Please feel free to contact me any time day or night when things develop or if there are any problems that you incur. When everything is finished, the military among our group will take charge of firing the prototype. Of course, that is with your supervision. They will conduct the initial firing of the weapon once you have it ready. Please instruct the sergeant working with your team about the firing procedure. We will test it outside the facility so that we do not chance damaging anything inside. No test will be conducted without my approval. Security, medics, and safety personnel must be present. Surely, you understand the need for these requirements, sir. Thank you. I will talk with you later, Dr. Piton. Keep up the good work, and please keep me posted," George requested with a smile.

George walked into his office with the smile still lingering. "Good morning, First Sergeant Collins."

Harry snapped to attention and replied, "Good morning, sir. You certainly look happy. Good news from Dr. Piton's team already?"

At that remark, the whole office paid attention.

"Yes, Harry, very good news. They may have had a breakthrough already. If it is truly a valid breakthrough that puts us ahead of schedule by at least a month."

Harry laughed. "That is great, Captain."

The room resounded with claps and cheers.

"Hold on, people, right now, we are just theorizing. Although I have the utmost confidence in Dr. Piton and his team, things are far from certain. We are in initial stages of drafting plans for completing our assignment and it may take considerably more time to accomplish any further progress. The engineers will have drawings to me within a week, and then you men will have a lot of work to do to get it assembled and prepared for its testing. However, Dr. Piton assured me that the future prospects look very promising and that things should work as planned.

Meanwhile, please keep a close lookout for any possible security breech. You know, like strange faces, someone you haven't seen around your area before. Watch for someone who may try to sabotage the equipment before we can test it. There could actually be spies in the camp, and we must not let them succeed in their plot. Everyone have a good and safe day."

George was tense with anticipation throughout the remainder of the day. Not only was his career on line, but countless American lives may be at stake.

*We must succeed*, he thought, then prayed, "Please, God, help us get this right the first time."

In his quarters that evening, he slept restlessly.

## Day 4

The next morning, Harry joined George as he walked toward his office. Dr. Piton met them.

"Gentlemen, I think we have had some success in finding the means to destroy the enemy's weapon."

George grabbed Dr. Piton's hand and gripped it so hard that he grimaced.

"Sorry, Doc, I'm just so excited that things are proceeding so well. What is the plan?"

Dr. Piton replied, "Well, Dr. Stakard believes that we can interfere with the firing process via a specially equipped satellite. I'm reasonably certain NASA will be able to attach it to an existing satellite. If not, we may have to send up a specially designed satellite for the new equipment array."

After Dr. Piton finished explaining the initial plan, George said, "That sounds great. Let me know the progress every two hours if you will, Doctor."

He responded, "As soon as I find anything new, I will apprise you of it immediately. If not, I will give you a report every two hours, sir."

"That'd be great. Thank you, Dr. Piton," George said as he turned to Harry, "Harry, I'm really excited about our progress. I believe that God is answering our prayers and blessing our efforts. At this rate, we may be able to stop the threat of that new weapon within three months or less."

Harry grabbed George's hand and said, "Congratulations, sir. You're right. God is blessing the work of our teams. But remember Murphy's Law and expect the unexpected, sir."

George replied, "Thanks, First Sergeant, I think. I do understand where you are coming from though. I would not be surprised if we have a hitch in our get-a-long at some point. But by God's grace, we will be able to resolve and overcome each of them."

No change was reported by Dr Piton during the rest of the day. George was thankful, at least for the fact that there was no bad news received. Near the end of the day, he made a visit to the lab. Dr. Mien Chan looked up from his work and greeted Captain Lee as he entered the engineering section, "Good afternoon, Captain. Things seem to be going very well. Dr. Piton is in his office entering data in the computer."

As George walked to Dr. Piton's office, he said, "Thank you, Dr. Chan. Keep up the good work. I will talk with you later."

He knocked on Dr. Piton's office door and heard a faint "Come in."

The doctor looked puzzled. "Captain, I'm not sure if some of the materials we need are readily available for our procurement."

"Well, give me a list and I will see if the Department of the Army can get them for us, Doctor," George advised.

"All right," Dr. Piton said, "I can print it out right now, if you would like to take it with you."

George looked happy. "Sure, Doctor. Is there something else I can help you with?"

Dr. Piton answered, "I can't think of anything at the moment, Captain."

The printer whirred into action as the list was printed. When the printer stopped, Dr. Piton gathered the papers and handed them to George. He examined the list after he got to his office. Dr. Piton's list looked reasonable so he used the secured fax to send them to HQ.

Near the end of the day, he decided to check with engineering and see what they thought of the list and also find out if they had made any further beneficial discoveries. Things seemed to be in order in the engineering section, so he decided to have an early dinner. He contacted Harry who agreed to join him.

Except for critically needed personnel, most everyone took Saturday (Day 4) off so most everyone could relax.

## Day 5

It was a standing order that Sunday was to be a day of rest and/or worship. Everyone would have the opportunity to attend worship services. No one seemed to be bothered by a day without the stress of work. Even the scientists had no problem with taking the day off. Many of them attended religious services. George sat listening to a good sermon from the book of Romans. The minister, Reverend Charles Clapp, talked about how everyone is born with the sin nature and ultimately has chosen to sin. Because of that, every person needs to be forgiven of their sinful deeds. While he was listening, George remembered that he was to meet with 1st Sergeant Collins before the evening service.

As he listened to the sermon, he simply could not help but to see if Laura Krieger was present. Sure enough, there she sat in her Sunday go-to-meeting dress. She looked so beautiful. He thought, *I am going to ask her to go with me to church this evening.*

At the close of the service, he waited for her at the door and asked her to walk with him to lunch.

She looked at him with curious eyes and asked, "Are you sure?" George did not understand that question, but before he could ask its meaning, Laura continued, "If you are, I certainly will have lunch with you."

He escorted her to the dining hall and opened the door for her. She led the way to the trays and they went through the chow line together. They sat across from each other and talked about their childhood. They laughed and enjoyed one another's company until he remembered that he needed to get some information to Sgt. Collins. He made his apologies to her and asked to be excused, but before he left the table, he told her, "Will you attend the evening service with me?"

She had a broad smile when she answered, "Oh, that would be great. I certainly did have a wonderful time during our lunch together."

George left with a gladdened heart.

George easily found Sergeant Collins and had a brief meeting with him about security. George informed him, "There will be a mail delivery by boat about 2400 hours tonight. Please make arrangements to have our mail delivered and theirs picked up when the submarine signals its location. And, Harry, please make sure that an announcement is made on the PA so that our personnel's mail can be ready in time. Also beef up Security for the mail pick-up. You might want to get with Lt. Dewitt so that you both will be on the same page. I will tell him to work with you."

After he left Harry, he contacted Lt. Dewitt about his talk with Sgt. Collins. That evening, George enjoyed the service, and afterward, he spent a pleasant time with Laura, then went to his quarters and read a good book as he listened to soft music playing on his stereo.

## Day 6

The next morning, George went to the gym before breakfast. Several soldiers and civilian personnel were working out. George decided that he would run. There actually was a running area that was approximately a mile long. After about eight laps, he decided that he would lift weights. As he added weights, someone noted how much he was lifting and quietly got the attention of many of the people nearby.

One of the men commented, "Captain, we are surprised at the amount of weight that you are lifting. You are lifting quite a lot for your size."

"I will take that as a compliment," Captain Lee said, "so thank you. Would you like to spot me?"

"I sure would. But I think I should get some help, just in case, you know, you have a problem," the young man replied.

"Thanks," he said as he prepared to lift the 200 pounds that he had placed on the bar.

The spotters stood on either side stayed ready to grab hold if the captain had any trouble. He did ten repetitions and then decided to add ten more pounds. He did only five of the 210 pounds and thanked the men for their help. As he left for the showers, he heard a ripple of comments among the men.

After a shower and a good breakfast, he went to the engineering section. The chief of this section was an engineer who had civil, mechanical, and computer engineering skills. The section was gathered around the chair of the chief engineer. They were discussing the available options relating to the guidance and delivery systems of electron particle beams, which the scientists had suggested as a means to enable the strike.

They failed to notice the captain until one of the men turned to retrieve an item from the table next to the desk where they were gathered.

The man turned to the group and stated, "Hey everyone, Captain Lee is here."

They almost in unison greeted him, "Good morning, Captain."

"Good morning, gentlemen and lady," Captain Lee replied. "What progress are you making?"

The chief rose from his seat with a smile and turned to the captain and shook his hand, "Captain, I am Mr. James Crenshaw, the chief engineer over this section. We are deciding on methods of delivery and what approach to use in containment of a particle beam, which the scientists are in the process of developing."

"Yes, Dr. Piton said he needed some parts to begin the chemical production that would combine with such a beam," George informed Mr. Crenshaw. "I have a list that I would like you to review and give your opinion about.

Would you and your team do that for me please? I will be back in a couple hours to check with you. Thanks for taking time for this."

As the captain turned to leave, Mr. Crenshaw replied, "Captain, I'm not sure we can be of any help with this list. At first glance, it looks like they should be the right things for their intended use. But we will certainly put our heads together and examine it."

George did not tell Mr. Crenshaw that he had already faxed the list to HQ.

The machinists had finished a few items, and the fabrication section had made enough parts that the assemblers were actually beginning to build the prototype of a miniature weapon they had discussed with Dr. Piton the day before. He took a look at the blueprints, and something caught his eye. He made a note of it so he could discuss it with the engineers. He took the number of the blueprint and the part number from the parts list in the upper right hand of the print so that he could find it in the original draft. He called the fabrication leader and the inspector over and instructed them not to start assembly of the items in question until they heard from engineering.

He left the fabrication shop and headed back to engineering. Mr. Crenshaw looked surprised to see the captain.

"You are back sooner than expected, Captain. We checked out the list of items you gave us to go over, and it seems to be in order. Is there something else?"

Captain Lee pulled the note from his pocket and gave Crenshaw the number of the print he had a question about. After the blueprint was spread out on the drafting table, he pointed out the parts in question and began, "Thanks. I have a concern about part numbers 27 and 28 on this print."

Mr. Crenshaw looked closely at the items, went over to his desk, and picked up a magnifying glass.

When he returned, he called to a member of his crew, "Come, and take a look at this print, Laura."

Laura approached the drafting table and studied the area that Crenshaw pointed out. "These will never work as drawn, Mr. Crenshaw."

Crenshaw asked Captain Lee, "Captain, have you met Laura Krieger? She is one of the brightest among our crew and knows the design of the mechanism better than anyone else in this room. We developed the plans together. Someone in drafting must have misunderstood our instructions and drew this in error."

The captain smiled. "Yes, Mr. Crenshaw, I have met Ms. Krieger, and it certainly my pleasure to see her again."

Laura had a slight blush as she responded, "Yes, Captain, and it is a pleasure to see you again as well."

The five feet ten inch tall blonde-haired beauty captivated George's attention. Her beautiful blue eyes made him have to focus on the situation at hand.

"Thank you, Laura."

She smiled and nodded as George turned back to Crenshaw. "Please see to it that these items are corrected." As he turned toward the door, he spoke quietly, "May I speak with you privately, Mr. Crenshaw?"

Crenshaw left the print with Laura and followed the captain to the door.

"Mr. Crenshaw, I'd appreciate it if you gave me the name of the draftsman who drew up these items and discretely follow his future work. Please check each print he draws with extra scrutiny and report any further errors to me ASAP. Everyone working here has had a background check, but we cannot afford to take any chances. You do understand how important this is, don't you?"

Crenshaw shook his head. "That thought had not occurred to me. The young man's name is Henry Davenport. He is a pleasant fellow, but I will keep an eye on him in the future and see if your fears are confirmed."

Captain Lee retired that evening with a concern over the parts errors and the young man who made them. But something better entered his mind before he drifted off to sleep. He envisioned the face of Laura Krieger as thoughts faded into a pleasant sleep.

## Day 7

First Sergeant Collins entered the captain's office the next morning, stood at attention, and saluted sharply, "Good morning, Captain Lee."

"Good morning, Harry," George greeted, "and by the way, please when we are alone, use my first name and drop the salute. I think we have been friends long enough and have such a strong professional relationship that it won't be a problem, don't you?"

"Sir, I respect you as an officer and a gentleman, and I would never do anything purposefully to disrespect you," Harry responded. And as an afterthought, "And that stands true in private or in public."

"Great," George responded, "I can tell you that I have the same feelings of respect about you. Now, what can I do for you this morning, Harry?"

"I just though I would give you a report on the morale of the men," Harry commented. "Things seem to be going well with all the crews, and the civilian and military personnel seem to have integrated without a hitch. There has been no problem between them. And I just wanted to know how you were getting along too."

George smiled. "Thanks, old friend. I guess I am doing well. I'm sure you miss Pam and Tommy. I know I miss my parents and my sister, Charlene. By the way, have you met an engineer by the name of Laura Krieger? You know the blonde that has those beautiful blue eyes."

Harry laughed. "Why, George, I think you got the bug. Are you running a fever? Your face is awfully flushed. To answer your question, yes, I have met her, and she definitely is a beauty. I heard her talking to some of the other girls at breakfast this morning. She was saying something about how handsome our commanding officer is. What do you think of that?"

"Makes me happy to know that," George replied. "We ate lunch together yesterday and she attended church service with me last night. She is so smart, and that scares me just a bit. I don't know if I could keep up with her, mentally speaking. It probably is too long a shot to work out any way. I certainly am looking forward to getting to know more about her, though."

"Yeah, I saw you two sitting together last night. Best of luck with this, and I will be sure keep my ears open for more news about her," Harry said with the biggest grin George had never seen across his face. "I think things would work out fine if you want my opinion. I had better be about my rounds. I will see you later, sir."

About that time, a knock at the office door interrupted them. Harry quickly rose and stood at the front of George's desk as George said, "Enter."

As the door opened, Harry stood at attention and requested to be excused.

"You are dismissed, Sergeant," George said.

Harry saluted and did an about-face and headed for the door. Dr. Piton entered the office. He and Sergeant Collins exchanged greetings as Harry left.

"I'm sorry to interrupt, Captain, but I thought you should know that the print errors have been corrected, and Henry Davenport has been doing excellent work since we started double-checking his work as you directed," Dr. Piton reported.

"Thank you, Dr. Piton," Captain Lee replied, "I'm relieved to hear that, but please continue to keep an eye on him and anyone that may have possibly changed the items after he did his drafting. Someone else may have tampered with them after Davenport completed them."

"I certainly will," Piton agreed. "Hey, how about having lunch, Captain. We could talk over lunch."

As Captain Lee and Dr. Piton headed for the mess hall, they chatted and got to know each other better. Dr. Piton asked George about his family and found out that he was not married.

"I heard down in engineering that you ate lunch with Laura Krieger. She would be a great catch. I know her family, and they are good people. They are highly respected in their community."

"She is a great looker," George said. "Man, and those beautiful eyes. I had an amazing lunch period with her."

"I might be able to put in a good word for you with her if you like, Captain," Mr. Crenshaw told George with a smile.

They finished their lunch, shook hands, and parted. As George made his rounds during the day, things were pretty much uneventful except for when he checked with engineering. He kept his eyes peeled for Ms. Krieger, but she was not working. George asked Mr. Crenshaw how Ms. Krieger was getting along, and he told him that she seemed to be having some kind of flu symptoms and had stayed in her room that day. George thanked him and told him he hoped she got to feeling better, and then excused himself.

# A MOLE AMONG THEM

## Day 8

George saw Laura Krieger sitting alone the next morning at breakfast. She glanced up as he headed for the trays at the breakfast buffet and stood and waved. George finished selecting his food and joined her at her table.

"Well, good morning, ma'am."

She smiled broadly and gave him a greeting hand.

"It seems you have recovered from the bug. I certainly am glad about that," George said sincerely.

Laura spoke with a slight lilt in her tone, "Yes, I'm feeling much better. And you certainly are looking good, Captain."

About that time, First Sergeant Collins entered the cafeteria. He hurriedly glanced around the room until he spotted George. He rushed over to the captain, stood at attention, and almost breathlessly said, "Captain, please come quickly, we have an emergency that needs your immediate attention."

George grabbed his donut and coffee, glanced at Laura, and told her that they would talk later. Laura had a concerned look as she watched George and Harry hurriedly leave the room. She wondered what the problem might be.

George followed Harry into the assembly area where men were standing around a piece of machinery.

"Captain, I'm sorry to have interrupted your breakfast, but I though you should see this," Mr. James Crenshaw said nervously.

"What's happening here, James?" George asked as he looked at the location receiving everyone's attention.

"Well, the fabrication crew called me and asked me to come and check on this. It appears that someone came in here last night and removed a critical item that we must have to test this machine, Captain," Mr. Crenshaw reported.

"First Sergeant, get security down here, and tell them I want to look at last night's security tapes ASAP. And, Harry, I would like you to come and watch the tapes with us."

The sergeant did an about-face and almost ran to the door. He returned in about five minutes with the head of security, First Lieutenant Patrick Dewitt.

"Sir, Lieutenant Dewitt reporting as ordered, sir."

"At ease, Lieutenant," George ordered. "Let's dispense with the formalities. Someone broke in here last night and removed a very important item. I want the base personnel confined to quarters until we find that item. Please have the security tapes ready for viewing ASAP, Lieutenant."

The Lieutenant saluted and told George, "Sir, the security sergeant was working on the tapes when I left the office. They are probably ready now."

George and Sergeant Collins followed Lt. Dewitt from the room. When they entered the security office, sure enough, the sergeant was screening the security tapes of the engineering area. Lt. Dewitt introduced Sergeant Decker to them.

"Sirs, this is probably going to take some time, but it looks the tapes are clear enough to identify the culprit or culprits," Sgt. Decker said.

Captain Lee responded, "Good work, Sgt. Decker. Will more men be needed?"

Sergeant Decker advised the captain, "Sir, I don't think so. I think Lt. Dewitt and I should be able to handle this. Besides, more people would simply get in our way."

Captain Lee told Lt. Dewitt, "Don't forget to have all nonessential personnel confined to quarters, and add an extra security detail to hallways and exits. And please have assembly department's exits security tapes checked as well as the assembly area tapes. If you need me, call my office. Let's get this person."

Complaints about being confined to quarters were coming into his office every few minutes, but George felt his actions were warranted. Finally, George got a call from Lt. Dewitt. He got Sgt. Collins to accompany him to the security office. As soon as they entered the security office, Lt. Dewitt motioned him to the monitors.

"Captain, take a look at this. About 0155, this man was seen entering the assembly area. I have already had him picked up. He is in the holding area. I thought you might want to see him or at least watch as he is being questioned. We have men searching his room as we speak."

"Good work, Lieutenant," George said. "May Sgt. Collins and I review the tape with you?" Sgt. Decker immediately began to replay the tape that showed the man entering the assembly. Ten minutes later, he exited the room carrying something. George asked the sergeant to zoom in on the item he was carrying. There it was, partially hidden by his shirt, the missing item. George motioned Harry.

"Harry, please go get Mr. Crenshaw and ask him to come with you to verify that this is, in fact, the missing item and the man I think it is."

It did not take long for Sgt. Collins to return with Mr. Crenshaw in tow. Mr. Crenshaw smiled as he looked at the screen. "That is it, sir. Thank God, you have found the missing item. Losing that would have caused us possibly a three-week delay."

George asked, "Who is the man carrying the item, Mr. Crenshaw?"

"I do believe that's Henry Davenport, the guy that messed up the prints on which you discovered the errors, sir," Crenshaw answered.

"Lt. Dewitt, take me to the room where Davenport is being held, please," George ordered. He followed the lieutenant down the hallway to the holding cell. Henry Davenport looked nervous as he stood to his feet as the two officers entered the room. George ordered him, "Sit down Henry!"

As he sat down, Davenport asked, "Wait, how did you know my name?"

George ignored the question. "We will ask the questions and you will do the answering. First, let me inform you that we have you on tape entering the assembly room after working hours. About ten minutes later, you left the assembly room carrying an item critical for testing the device from that room. Where is it?"

Henry Davenport tried to look innocent. "I have no idea what you are talking about, Captain."

"Oh, I think you do, son," George replied. "Let me ask you another question. Have you ever heard of water boarding?"

Davenport nodded in the affirmative. "Well, I have a first sergeant that has had experience in that area. He is an expert in interrogation techniques, and I'm sure he is most eager to hone his skills in other techniques he has learned from some of his ranger friends. I will give you one more opportunity to talk before I send him in. Neither Lt. Dewitt nor I will be here to stop him after he begins working with you. There will be no one to hear your screams. Now, what do you say, son? Will you talk to us now, or do you want to meet my first sergeant?"

There was a long silence before Davenport spoke, "Sir, I think you are bluffing."

George stood and motioned for Lt. Dewitt to follow, "You can't say I did not warn you, Mr. Davenport. I'm sorry, but there will be no flowers for your grave, and your family will never know what happened to you. Good-bye, Henry Davenport. Whether you talk or not, we will find the part you have stolen from that room."

Lt. Dewitt opened the door for the captain, and they headed out of the room.

Before they had closed the door, George called First Sergeant Collins, "Would you come down and question Mr. Henry Davenport for us? He has not been very cooperative."

Sergeant Collins answered, "Sir, I will need my equipment. Let me have time to go get my tools, I will be right back."

"Wait, Captain," Davenport yelled as Sergeant Collins approached the cell door, "I will tell you what you want to know."

"Sergeant Collins, please get your tools and come into the room just in case Mr. Davenport has a change of heart about telling us what we need to know," George said with a wink at Harry.

It did not take long to get the information they needed and to retrieve the missing item and take it back to Mr. Crenshaw's waiting hands. George had Lt. Dewitt rescind the "confinement to quarters" order, and soon, everything was back to normal.

The captain walked to the assembly area to confirm that the pulsation device had been given to Mr. Crenshaw. While he was there, he requested that Laura be excused to accompany him back to the cafeteria and finish the breakfast and the conversation they had started.

Laura smiled as she approached the captain. "I'm pretty busy, but I suppose we may go and finish breakfast during lunch. I see that the pulsation device has been retrieved. Who took it?"

"I'm sorry, but I can't divulge that information, but I think that you probably have a good idea who it was," George commented as he escorted Laura back to the dining room. Not many people were in the cafeteria so they could talk privately. Laura and George talked about their childhood and their parents and siblings. Finally, the captain was paged to report to the office. He excused himself and they said their good-byes and went their separate ways.

Lt. Dewitt was waiting in his office. "We have attained information from Davenport that I thought you would need to know immediately, sir. The news makes me very nervous, sir."

"What is it, Lieutenant?" George questioned.

"Davenport told us that he is working for a consortium that includes Asian and Arabian nations. This thing must be big, sir."

"Yes, and the consequences of not eliminating this threat will be huge. Thank you, Lieutenant, you did a great job. I will need to get this information to headquarters," he advised as he picked up the red phone in his office.

Colonel John Murphy had just finished a meeting when the major reported that there was a call on the secure line in his office. He thanked the major and hurried to the phone.

"Hello Captain Lee, how is it going out there?"

George reported the effort to conceal the stolen item and the information he had gotten from Davenport and the lieutenant to the colonel. Then Colonel Murphy informed him that when the mail drop was made that Davenport was to be ferried back to the submarine.

"There will be armed escorts for the prisoner." Then he ordered, "Make sure that he gets on that boat. Do you have or need anything else, George?"

George told the colonel that there was nothing else to report or that he needed. "Good work, Captain. Keep me informed."

Arrangements were made by Lt. Dewitt for his MP platoon to deliver Davenport to the shore for transport out to the sub when Sergeant Collins's man picked up the mail from the mainland.

George reminded Sergeant Collins, "Please alert the facility that mail may be sent at that time."

## A Surprise Romance

### Day 9

Laura smiled as she joined George for breakfast.

"Good morning, Captain Lee. You look handsome this morning." She had a gleam in her eye that George had not noted before.

"Good morning to you, Laura Krieger," George smiled back, "and I just want to know why you look so, what shall I call it? Would it be chipper?"

"Oh, for no reason, I just have good feelings this morning, and seeing you walk into the room made me feel even better," Laura responded with a sheepish grin.

George's heart rate elevated slightly as he looked into Laura's smiling face. They took their food to a table and sat talking about the progress being made. She watched George and wondered, *I hope I did not scare him off by acting like a teen with a crush.*

George sat across from her, thinking, *Wow. I hope I didn't put her off by acting as though I did not notice her romantic overtures.*

Both of them avoided pursuing that line of conversation. At the ending of the meal, Laura accompanied him as far as the engineering section.

George asked her, "Before I leave you, would you consider going with me to the movie showing in the media room this evening?"

Laura looked up into his face. "Captain, are you asking me for a date?"

"Yes, I am," George said, smiling down at her. "My, you are certainly beautiful. Sorry. I got distracted."

Laura quickly reached up and gave him a kiss. "I hope that answers your question."

George quickly said, "I will stop by your quarters about 1830 hours. Okay then."

Headquarters contacted George and informed him that they had gotten more valuable information from Mr. Davenport.

Colonel Murphy greeted George, "Good morning, Captain Lee. I will be sending you a package meant for your eyes only on the sub that is to arrive on or about 2400 hours. Make sure security is tight, and that all personnel keep their eyes and ears open for other clandestine operatives that may be active in or around the installation."

George reported that he had already taken action to tighten security and that the device would be ready for testing within a couple days if all went as planned. The colonel thanked George and asked if he would give his regards to Dr. Piton. George consented, and without further conversation, the colonel ended the call.

The rest of the day went smoothly and there was progress on the project. George had dinner delivered to his quarters. He did not want to stop reviewing the reports from the various department leaders. The call to Lt. Dewitt verified that plans were in place to deliver the mail along with Davenport over to the HQ team and pick up the mail from the mainland and take special precautions with the document being sent to him by the HQ crew. One glance at his watch, and George dropped everything, walked over to the mirror, and checked out the image in the mirror.

Laura was reading a book while waiting in her quarters. When the captain knocked at her door, she opened it.

"Wow, you look so gorgeous." George hardly got those words out because he was so enthralled by her beauty.

"You clean up pretty nice too, mister," Laura responded. "Do you know, for a captain, you certainly are shy." George was still staring when she grabbed his arm and said, "Okay, let's go, Mr. Shy Guy."

# Day 10

When he went to his office the next morning, George saw the note for him to come to the security office and pick up the document that was delivered from HQ. He hurried to the security section and entered.

Lt. Dewitt reached the document to him as he said, "Hello, Captain Lee."

George responded, "Good morning, how is it going, Lieutenant? How was Davenport when you transferred him to the HQ squad?"

"Captain, it was strange. He actually looked pleased to be going with them. I just could not believe his reaction. He seemed to be relieved to be handed over to HQ Security. Anyway, here is the document they delivered last evening, sir."

"Thanks, Lieutenant, do you mean he looked happy about the situation. I agree, that does seem strange," George agreed. "Do you think that he may be working with someone in the squad? Perhaps I had better contact HQ again. What do you think?"

Lt. Dewitt answered, "I have my suspicions, and yes, I do think you need to report this to HQ, sir."

Captain Lee headed for his office. He sat down and reached for the phone, but decided to check out the correspondence from HQ first. He opened the envelope stamped "Top Secret—For Captain George Lee's Eyes Only" in red. As he read the letter, a smile appeared across his face. It stated that Henry Davenport was working undercover to check out how he and the security section would handle a security breach. The colonel commended Captain Lee and Lt. Dewitt on how they had handled the situation with Davenport and added, "Please relay our thanks to Lt. Dewitt for his professionalism. I just heard how you used the threat of torture on Davenport, and he actually was scared for his safety and was happy that he was not really a spy because you had convinced him that Sgt. Collins would do him harm."

George thought, *Well, Davenport was right. Harry would have done what was necessary to get information out of him. Lt. Dewitt's suspicions were correct about the Davenport transfer to HQ.*

George picked up the phone and asked to be connected to security.

Sgt. Decker answered the phone, "Security, Sgt. Decker."

"Sgt. Decker, this is Captain Lee. Would you have Lt. Dewitt report to my office when he has time?" Sgt. Decker agreed. George thanked Decker and placed the phone back on the cradle.

In about ten minutes, Lt. Dewitt entered the office. George invited him to have a seat and then showed the communication to him. Like George, the lieutenant smiled as he read the document, "I just knew something was fishy, the way Davenport was behaving. I'm glad you were able to convince him to talk. That threat to use Sgt. Collins worked very well."

"I'm certainly glad that Davenport talked because it was really not a bluff. Sgt. Collins is well qualified to do exactly what I threatened Davenport with." They both had a chuckle over that as George continued, "I am glad the first sergeant was not forced to use such methods. It might not have been appreciated by HQ. But I guess alls well that ends well, huh?"

## Day 11

George visited Engineering to meet with Dr. Charles Piton, Dr. Stakard, both scientists, and Mr. James Crenshaw, the lead engineer. They were prepared to discuss the function of the pulsation device and how it would be utilized in destroying the capability of the enemy's weapon. They would also discuss how the device would be integrated into the machine when it was completed.

When George arrived, the men were chatting.

Dr. Piton said, "Good morning, Captain. We have been discussing the pulsation device. Let me catch you up to speed on our information. First, we think we can utilize the particle accelerator to supplement the pulsation device. The device will be bombarded with a steady stream of particles produced by an electromagnetic beam directed through the pulsation device. The pulsation device will stop the particles for a nanosecond. The result should build enough energy into the particles that when the particles are discharged, the blast should annihilate the target. A failure to control the amount of energy build-up in the pulsation device could possibly destroy the equivalent of a whole city block. That means a major portion of the facility."

George asked, "Do you think this is about ready to test fire?"

The scientists believed they were, but Mr. Crenshaw seemed hesitant.

"Why do you hesitate to agree, Mr. Crenshaw?" George asked.

"Well, sir," Crenshaw replied, "we are not yet certain that the particle accelerator shielding is adequate to contain the electrons and positrons. I believe that the photons and gluons for the field quanta will be no problem."

Dr. Stakard said, "But, Mr. Crenshaw, neither the leptons nor quarks should be a problem for the shielding we have already designed for the device. We both know that the matter, when propelled out of the accelerator, should be contained in a beam no larger in diameter than the size of a 90 MM cannon projectile."

"Yes, Dr. Stakard, but what about when the pulse device is restricting the electrons and positrons before it is propelled on toward the target?" Mr. Crenshaw retorted.

George interceded, "All right, gentlemen, let me ask you this. Is there any way to test the shielding before we actually test-fire the unit?"

Dr. Piton looked contemplative. "Yes, but it would take a couple extra days to get it ready."

"Okay, gentlemen," George said decisively, "here is what we will do. We will use the same materials with the same cellular configuration as the device casing and test it with that installed. Let's get this thing tested to quell any concerns that Mr. Crenshaw has. Thank you, gentlemen, let me know when the shield is ready for testing. Make sure that you have the proper testing equipment ready. If you need anything that would expedite the testing, let me know. Have a great day, everyone."

As George turned to leave, Laura was entering the office. "Hey, beautiful. How is your day going?"

Laura smiled. "Well, thank you, you handsome dude, I am doing quite well today. How did your meeting go?"

"Actually, I think we came up with a plan: testing the shielding for the accelerator and the pulsation device to assure that it is adequate to protect the firing crew," George replied.

"I walked by the office earlier, and they were really in deep conversation," Laura commented.

George looked serious. "If you have any ideas that would hasten this testing, it will be greatly appreciated. By the way, may I have the pleasure of your company this evening during and after dinner?"

"Why, sir, I would be delighted to have dinner and afterglow with you," Laura answered as she looked deeply into his eyes.

He turned to leave as he said, "Great. I will see you at dinner."

At his office, George contacted Harry and asked him to meet him in his office. Harry reported to the office in about ten minutes and did the military thing. George stood and shook his hand and invited him to be seated.

"How are you, Harry? I have been so busy that I haven't had time to talk with you. I invited you here so that I can give you a heads-up that we are planning to test the shielding of the accelerator and pulsation units. Please find out as much as you can about what the effects of a shield failure would be and how the thing works. Perhaps Laura Krieger may be able to help you."

Harry smiled. "I understand, and I will learn all I can. You know, boss, I think that she just might be the reason you don't have much time. What do you say, George?"

"Well, Harry, I think you may be on to something there," George said, with a glow on his face. "She seems like a great girl. She has brains, looks, and a great personality. I'm trying to be cautious, but she could push me over the edge with just a little nudge."

Harry laughed. "George, you have got it bad. Let me take your pulse."

George laughed and waved his hand to stop Harry, "Okay, enough of that. Harry, I have something to tell you that you need to keep under your hat. No one is to know about this except Lt. Dewitt, you and I. In fact, neither of you are supposed to know, so please do not divulge this to anyone. Do you remember Davenport?"

"I sure do. He was a spy," Harry responded.

"That's what I want to tell you about," George interrupted. "He was an HQ plant. They placed him here to test our security. Can you believe that, Harry?"

"Well, I'll be, sir," Harry said, shaking his head. "I am sure glad that I didn't have to use my questioning techniques on him. That may not have gone over too well with the brass."

"I know," George said with a serious look. "But he was convinced that you would have, and I'm certainly glad he told us something even if it was a lie. Harry, let me know what you learn about this shielding as often as needed."

Harry excused himself and agreed, "Okay, George, and I'll keep you up-to-date on that pretty engineer lady too." He hurriedly left the room when George acted as though he was going to throw a notebook at him.

## WEDDING BELLS?

Laura and George had a terrific dinner together, and then they went over to the Sky Room because it had a great view of the stars. They were both in relaxed mood, and before they knew it, they were cuddling together. George could not resist putting his arm around Laura. She responded by moving closer.

"Wow, George, this is nice. I cannot believe that you and I have become so close in just a few short days."

"I know we haven't known each other very long, but I think you have won my heart, Laura," George whispered. "You are the most beautiful woman that I have ever met. At least, you are the most beautiful woman that has ever had anything to do with me."

They both laughed as Laura reached up and pulled George's head toward hers and kissed him with a lingering kiss.

Laura said, "George, I think I have fallen for you too. What are we going to do about it? I was hoping to take my boyfriend to meet my parents before we married."

George hesitated. "I had not thought of that. I wanted to take my girlfriend home to meet my parents before I tied the knot too. Do you think we can wait until the project is finished? Wait. Let's not get ahead of ourselves. I had not planned on this happening tonight, or I would have found some way to get a ring." He suddenly rose, turned toward her, and then dropped down on one knee and asked, "Will you marry me, Laura Krieger?"

She smiled and grabbed him around his neck. "I certainly will, Captain George Lee. You know, George, we do have a chaplain here, don't you? We could talk to him about performing the ceremony and I could move into your quarters. Wouldn't that be great?"

"If you want, I will check with him tomorrow first thing," George said as he smothered her with kisses between words.

Laura objected, "No. Not tomorrow, let's talk to him tonight. How about it, honey?"

George pulled her up toward him and kissed her once again. "Hey! Wait! We need a license, don't we?"

"We can talk to him about that, too, George," Laura prompted.

They left the Sky Room and headed toward the chaplain's quarters. George knocked on his door nervously. It seemed like half an hour to him, but the chaplain finally opened the door.

"Good evening, Captain Lee, I was just having my devotions. What can I do for you, and…oh, hi, Ms. Krieger."

"Reverend Clapp, I know it's late, but we have a question for you about the need of a marriage license so we can get married here on this island. Do we need one? Can you perform the ceremony for us?" George's words almost ran together because he was so nervous.

"Well, Captain," Rev. Clapp responded thoughtfully. "Out here, the situation is like that of a ship, the captain of the ship can sign the paperwork and the ceremony can take place. Do you know the man in charge of this island, Captain Lee?"

George was so shook up that he could not think straight.

Laura laughed and said, "Honey, you are! You are the commanding officer of the island, so you can sign the proper papers."

Rev. Clapp chuckled and said, "I just happen to have the proper papers in my filing cabinet in the chapel office. You will still need two witnesses. If you can get them, we can do it right now if you would like."

George asked, "Laura do you have anyone you would like to stand as a witness and a bridesmaid?

Laura said, "Yes. You get your man and I'll get a friend from the engineering section to stand up with me."

Rev. Clapp agreed to have the necessary paperwork in the chapel within fifteen minutes. George went to get Harry, and Laura went to get her friend.

Harry opened his quarter's door to see a nervous friend shaking like a leaf. "What's the matter, Captain?"

With a shaky voice, George asked, "Harry, would you stand as my best man and as a witness of Laura's and my wedding tonight?"

With a broad smile and a chuckle, Harry grabbed the captain and yelled, "I knew it! I just knew it. I knew you had been bitten by that love bug. Congratulations. Let me change into my uniform, and you had better get into your best uniform as well, Captain."

"I never thought of that," George yelled as he turned toward his room. "Thanks, Harry! Please meet us in the chapel in about twenty minutes. Okay?"

It took a little longer than expected, but after the paperwork had been filled out, they finally gathered in front of the chapel's altar. The chaplain prayed for the couple about to be joined in the bonds of holy matrimony. Since there were no rings, the wedding was short. Laura had changed into a beautiful dress. Her bridesmaid stood by her side. It was a beautiful ceremony. Laura had tears as George said his vows to her. She actually wept as she recited her vows to George. Rev. Clapp pronounced them husband and wife and then offered a prayer for God's blessings on their future together. Pictures were taken by the chaplain, and then Harry took one of George and Laura standing before the chaplain. Several pictures were taken so they could be sent to their relatives.

Harry and Amy, Laura's friends, and the chaplain all congratulated the newlyweds.

Harry told them, "I will have extra copies of the pictures made for each one of you. I should have them done in a couple days. Laura, I will see you tomorrow." He shook hands with and saluted the captain, then said, "Congratulations, sir. I hope you and Laura have a wonderful evening." He left chuckling under his breath.

As they left the chapel, George said, "Your place or mine, honey?"

The chaplain and Amy heard him and the four of them had a big laugh together.

Laura said, "I've never slept in the captain's quarters before, so let's go to your place. We can stop by my quarters and I will pick up some things I will need to take with me. I love you, George."

George smiled. "I love you too. I think you have made this the happiest day of my life, Laura Krieger Lee."

Laura smiled. "It just might get happier, honey."

They stopped by her quarters so Laura could pick up some items she would need that night and clothing that she would need for work the next morning.

# Day 12

When the newlyweds entered the cafeteria the next day, everyone inside yelled out in unison, "Congratulations," as the mess sergeant carried out a wedding cake and sat it on one of the tables. Even the chaplain was there.

Sgt. Collins walked over to the table and said, "Captain, I wish you and Mrs. Lee many happy years together. May your marriage be as happy as Pamela's and mine."

George stood and gave Harry a hug. "Thanks, old friend, I hope so too. I appreciate you both as a friend and professional, Harry."

It seemed that all the facility's personnel were present. Lt. Dewitt led the line that formed to congratulate the newlyweds. The atmosphere was cheerful as George and Laura ate their breakfast. When George finally got a moment to talk with Laura alone, he said, "I just had a thought. We should let our parents know that we have married, Laura."

Laura agreed, "Actually, I had planned to write and let both sets of parents know about it and send them copies of the wedding pictures. We can send them when HQ makes the next mail run. If I remember correctly, it may even be tonight."

"I'll ask Harry if he can get the pictures ready on time," George agreed.

After breakfast, he and Laura went about their duties. George phoned HQ and they told him that the mail would be arriving the next evening at 2400 hours. George told the colonel that he was really surprised that Davenport was a plant.

Colonel Murphy told him, "Davenport is one of our best. You really had him convinced that your sergeant was going to use some form of torture technique on him. That was ingenious, George."

"Colonel, I have some happier news, Laura Krieger and I were married last night."

The colonel's reaction was one of joy. "Well, George, I thought you were destined for bachelorhood, but congratulations. I wish you the best. I will send the necessary paperwork to get her designated as your beneficiary. Better still, I will send two sets of papers, one for your signature and another for her making you her beneficiary."

"One more thing, sir," George put in, "we will be running tests on the shielding for the particle accelerator and the pulsation device as soon as we are sure that we can run the tests safely."

"Captain, that's great news." The colonel was happy about that. "Make sure you let me know and advise me of when we can expect an actual test firing of the machine."

"Sir, if it's possible, I will try to make them one and the same so that testing the shields will actually be a test firing of the weapon as well."

The colonel said, "Hold on, there is one more thing. You should let your parents know about the wedding."

"We are sending out letters on the sub tomorrow night, sir," George returned. "Our parents should know after they get the letters and a few pictures. Thanks for the advice." That ended the conversation as both said their good-byes.

Dr. Piton came into George's office. "Captain, I think we are set to test the shielding whenever Sgt. Collins gets all the safety equipment set up."

"That's terrific, Doctor," George replied with excitement in his voice. "Doctor, let me run something by you." Dr. Piton looked intently at George as he continued with a question. "Do you think it is possible to set up some kind of target so that we may combine the firing test with the shield testing?"

The doctor's face lit up.

"That's an excellent idea. Let me get our group together and discuss this as the safety team sets up the equipment," the doctor replied.

"Include Sgt. Collins in this discussion," George instructed. "I will be there in just a few minutes. Thanks, Doctor."

Before he left, he called HQ and let the colonel know that they were about to test the shielding and would most likely use a target as well. After he finished talking with Murphy, he headed for the testing site.

As he opened the door to the outside, he saw that the camouflage matched the surrounding foliage and that Sgt. Collins and his men were setting up a target made of what appeared to be a series of pieces of steel each about four inch thick. He walked over to the group standing in a huddle.

"Good morning, ladies and gentlemen. Are we nearly set up and about ready to go?"

Dr Piton turned and addressed George, "Captain Lee, we decided to implement your idea. After all, why use the test firing just to test the shielding when we can utilize it to check the destructive power of the beam as well."

"Thanks for getting it set up, Doctor. Where is the designated observation area? Will there be anything noticeable above the camouflage when the target is destroyed?"

"Unfortunately, Captain, we are uncertain as to what to expect," Dr Piton began. "We anticipated the possibility of setting the jungle vegetation ablaze, so we tried to set up deflector shields behind the target's position as well as behind the weapon. Beyond that, it is anyone's guess. This test has never been attempted before."

# What a Blast

Sgt. Collins entered the room where they were waiting and reported to Dr. Piton, "I think we have set up everything according to your specs, sir."

Dr. Piton motioned everybody toward a small hut that had been erected just for this occasion. Inside were gauges and instruments to measure the amount of radiation passing through the integrated shielding device.

Dr. Piton pressed a button and a warning siren sounded. After that, a computerized countdown counted backward. "10, 9, 8…"

As the countdown continued, Dr. Piton looked over at George and asked, "Captain, would you like to do the honors?"

George shook his head. "No, Doctor, you go. It's your baby." Immediately, at the end of the countdown, Dr. Piton pushed the button and there was a weird shrill piercing sound and a thunder-like clap that jarred the building as the blast shattered the targets. The shield beyond the targets had a darkened area about the size of the old-fashioned laundry tubs that grandmas used to use to give the grandkids their Saturday night baths in. George watched the gauges. Some moved slightly while others jumped almost to the maximum peg stop. Dr. Piton looked pleased.

"Captain, those gauges that moved very little were the ones that indicated the integral shielding was holding while the ones that jumped and pegged out were the ones that received readings from sensors that were set up in the open area beyond the exit of the particles as it exited the mechanism and at the target area. It appears that both the testing of the shielding and the test firing were successful. One more thing, the device didn't move an inch. It's amazing."

George and Dr. Piton shook hands as cheers rang out from others in the hut, "Congratulations, Doctor." Then he walked over to Harry and shook his hand. After that, he walked to where Laura stood smiling and gave her a big warm hug.

"Honey, it worked. I'm so proud of everyone." He raised his voice. "Hey, everyone, you all did a terrific job with this project. It should be a downhill coast from here. But for now, I think we should all go to the dining room. I don't think Sergeant Grant would mind serving some ice cream and pop. Dr. Piton, make sure we have the results of these readings ready to send with the mail tomorrow night. Also, send a DVD of the test along with the recordings and their meanings. Right now, please take them to your office. After that, please join us in the cafeteria."

Dr. Piton grabbed his laptop and headed toward the door as most of the team's members stood discussing what they had just witnessed.

Laura walked with George to the cafeteria. Sgt. Grant had already planned the celebration, so he had several servings of ice cream and pop and cookies set out for the celebration. "Captain, there's also coffee and tea, if anyone would like that."

"Thank you, Allen. I hope this is not too much trouble. I really do appreciate you doing this."

Laura and he took a few minutes to celebrate with the boisterous crowd and then George told her, "I need to get this information to HQ ASAP, so if you will excuse me, I'll go let them know the results of the testing."

"George, I don't think I will be working any more today, so why don't I come with you," Laura whispered. "When you are done, we can go to our quarters and do some private celebrating by ourselves. What do you think about that?"

George mouthed his reply, "Just follow me."

He excused himself, although most did not notice their departure.

At the office, he picked up the red phone. He heard the phone ring on the other end and Colonel Murphy say, "Hello, George. What's happening out there? We saw satellite readings that indicated there was some sort of major explosion on the island. Did it work?"

"That's what I am calling about, sir," George said with excitement. It appears that the shields held and it made holes through a series of four four-inch steel targets. They were demolished. We had deflector shields set up, just in case the beam was not stopped by the target. It was a good thing that we did because the mechanism fired through approximately three and one half feet diameter and left that big of a burn mark on the deflector. It appeared successful to us, but we will sent you a copy of the results and recordings of the testing with tomorrows mailing."

"This is exciting news, Captain Lee. We have been working on getting a satellite adapted to mate with it so we can place this thing in orbit. If this is as successful as you seem to believe, we will have this thing up in orbit within the next couple weeks. Oh yes, I contacted Laura's parents. At first, they were pretty upset, but when I told them what a fine catch you were, they calmed down. They will be happy to get the letter and pictures from you guys. Good day, George. I think it's time for a celebration."

George thanked the colonel for the kind words and informed him that the celebration was already in full swing. When he hung up the phone, he grabbed Laura and gave her a big kiss, and led her through the door. They walked down the hallway toward their quarters hand in hand.

*What a perfect ending to a perfect day*, George thought as they neared their room.

## Problems in Paradise

### Day 13

"Sunday, another day of worship and R and R," George told Laura as he reached across and took her hand.

Still holding his hand, she stood and walked around and sat on George's lap.

"Dear, it looks like this project may be completed soon, and our lives may take on a bit of normalcy. I don't even know what kind of car you have, so please tell me."

"Well," George began, "I do not own a vehicle, and it's been so long since I have used my driver's license, I don't know if it has expired or not. I do have a military driver's license. I even have a license to drive a tank."

"Are you serious?" Laura asked. "Do you mean you may not have a license to drive a civilian car, but you have a tank driver's license?"

"Sure enough," George said with a chuckle. "I have had Harry assigned as my driver for the past year, so I really had no need for a vehicle, and therefore no need to use my driver's license. Do you own a vehicle?"

Laura smiled. "Why, yes I do. I own a Cadillac CTS. It has a few years on it, but it still is a great ride. I really like it. It's parked at Mom's and Dad's."

"Well, I have preferred Lincolns, like an MKX, so I don't have to duck down to get into it. But I sold my vehicle when I was deployed overseas," George told Laura.

They finished the conversation when Laura decided that she would drive George around in her CTS as they walked toward the cafeteria. The breakfast aroma wafted in the air outside the cafeteria, and by the time Laura and George opened the mess hall door, their taste buds were bursting with anticipation. Laura licked her lips.

"Man, this smells like down-home cooking. Keep your eye on me, and don't allow me to eat so much that I will sleep during church service."

"Oh, I have kept an eye on you ever since the first time I met you. Beautiful lady," George replied with a twinkle in his eye, "as your commanding officer, it will be my duty to keep an eye on you for the rest of our lives."

Their trays were full as they walked over to Harry's table and asked if they could sit with him. He nodded and they seated themselves.

"Good morning, Harry," George began, "you certainly look good today."

Harry thanked him and asked how they were doing. Then George asked about Pam and Tommy, "Did you hear from them this last mail drop?"

Harry looked a bit concerned. "Yes, and both Pam and the baby seem to have flu symptoms."

"That's too bad, Sgt. Collins," Laura said with a troubled look. "Did they have high temps?"

Harry nodded. "I believe Pam said her temperature got up to 102. They went to the infirmary, and both got shots. So they both are probably doing better by now."

George told Harry, "I hope so. Laura and I will pray for him."

They all finished their breakfast and returned to their rooms. George and Laura left Harry at his door after they agreed to meet at the service at 1000 hours. As they continued toward their room, there was a distant sound of a rumble of some sort. At their depth beneath the camouflaged covering, they could not distinguish it as the sound of thunder. However, as the frequency of the thunder increased, it became obvious that they were having a storm. This was something that George had not counted on. Not just because it was what he referred to as the

Lord's Day, but because he believed that "all things work together for good to those who love the Lord, to those who are called according to His purpose." As they neared the chapel entrance.

George looked over at Laura and said, "I am not going to worry about this storm. We will just trust in God to take care of this facility and these that are working here."

The Reverend Charles Clapp took his text from John 14:1–3 (kjv). He read, "Let not your heart be troubled: ye believe in God, believe also in me. In my Father's house are many mansions: if *it were* not *so*, I would have told you. I go to prepare a place for you. And if I go and prepare a place for you, I will come again, and receive you unto myself; that where I am, *there* ye may be also."

Rev. Clapp preached an encouraging message about believers being taken away (raptured) at the time that their Savior, the Lord Jesus Christ, returns to claim them as His own. He closed the sermon by encouraged someone to come forward and receive the soon returning Christ as their Savior. Unfortunately, no one responded. George told Rev. Clapp how much his message meant to him.

Then the chaplain asked, "How are the two newlyweds doing?"

Laura answered, "Let me answer that question, Brother Clapp. George has made this the happiest few days of my life. I thank God every morning that he is the man he is and that I am fortunate enough to be his bride."

George followed suit with "And I can claim that about her as well. And with God in our lives, I think we can face life together and have the hope that this will not change."

"Wow, what a testimonial from the both of you," Charles Clapp responded. "I haven't heard but maybe three other couples make these sorts of comments about their marriage during my whole ministry. How blessed you two are."

About that time, the lights went out and some of the women screamed. George took control.

"Does anyone have a lighter?"

One of the fellows from the assembly crew yelled from inside the chapel as a small light came on, "I have one of those lights that come with a key chain."

To his amazement, several others had small lights. "All right, how about the ones with the lights escort this group to the area where we tested the mechanism while I go to my quarters and radio the office and find our status. Will one of you be so kind as to lead me to my quarters? Okay, let's go, and be very careful."

Sgt. Collins and George followed a young man to the captain's quarters. The emergency exit lights kicked on by the time they got to his room. George found a flashlight and thanked Kevin, a lab tech, for showing him back to his quarters. Harry and he were headed toward the security office when the lights came back on. Lt. Dewitt looked up as they entered the office.

"What happened, Lieutenant?" George asked.

"Sir, somehow, water got into the diesel fuel and that's why the generator failed," Dewitt replied. "It is like a monsoon out there, Captain."

George asked, "Really?"

"Yes, sir, it's raining cats and dogs. I guess you could say it's raining horses and cattle, it's coming down so hard," Lt. Dewitt said with a smile.

"I guess you took care to keep this from occurring again, didn't you?" George asked.

"Well, sir, there was a water leak that somehow may have drained into the reserve tank of the generator," Dewitt explained. "Somehow, the polluted fuel got over into the supply tank. The maintenance crew drained the fuel from the tanks and filtered out the water and replaced the fuel filters and poured enough fuel back into the tank to get the generator started and get the lights back on. When I left, they were preparing to top off the tank."

"Great work," George commended Lt. Dewitt. "Let's go and thank the maintenance crew now."

They left the security office and headed toward the maintenance room.

"Hi, Sam," George greeted. "How are you?"

"Good evening, Captain Lee and Lieutenant Dewitt," Sam Salway said. "We were just fine until the lights went out, but I think we have that taken care of that."

Captain Lee told Sam, "Yeah, we were just getting out of church when they went off."

Salway looked up. "Yes, sir, I saw you and your new bride there. I was in the back with one of my crew members during the service. By the time we got to the office, one of our crew had found the problem."

George shook Sam's hand. "That's the reason I stopped by. I wanted to thank you and your crew for a job well done, Sam."

"Well, they are in the next room, so let's go tell them," Sam suggested.

"Sure," George smiled as he followed Sam through an open door into the next room. Sam advised the captain that these were the men and woman who had taken fast action to get the generator going so quickly.

George began, "Lt. Dewitt reported how you worked so hard to get the electricity back on so quickly, so I just wanted to come here and thank you personally for a job well executed. Thank each of you for fixing our problem and hopefully prevent it from happening again. Have a great Lord's Day afternoon, everyone. Thanks again for the great work you did." He took time to shake everyone's hand and personally thank them before they all went to lunch.

George asked Sam to walk with him a bit. Sam looked inquisitive as he joined the captain.

"The reason I asked you to walk with me is that I wanted to ask you about the possibility of someone intentionally causing the problem with the generator."

Sam looked startled at the suggestion. "Well, I had not considered that possibility, but I will take a closer look and let you know what I find out, Captain."

"After the incident in the assembly area, I thought it may be feasible for that to happen," George put in. "And please expedite this ASAP, we are getting near the completion of the project, and we don't want anything to jeopardize making that happen. Please stay alert. Thanks ahead of time."

As George entered the cafeteria, he saw Laura sitting so that the light accented her long golden hair. She looked over at George with those gorgeous blue eyes and a smile that revealed her pearly white teeth and his heart melted. "My, how fortunate I am to have a wife that is so beautiful." He waved as he headed toward her.

"Hi, honey," Laura said as he neared, "what was the problem?"

"It seems that water somehow leaked into the reserve fuel tank and caused the engine to fail," George explained. "May I join you for lunch?"

"Of course, silly," Laura laughed. They went over to pick up a tray, and when George thought no one was looking, he sneaked a kiss from Laura. "George, that was sweet. We will have to practice that more in our room after lunch."

Fortunately, the rest of the day was uneventful.

# Day 14

After George got to his office, HQ called, and after the usual courtesies, Colonel Murphy told George, "Captain Lee, the division commander, General Commodore has instructed us to send a satellite so that your people can mount the mechanism to it. The satellite mounting brackets were adapted utilizing prints of the mechanism. Along with it are the prints for mounting those brackets, so that if there any changes necessary, you may note them on the drawings when the mechanism is mounted to the satellite. Once the mounting is completed, we will arrange to get you off that island and back to the mainland. Please expedite this as quickly as possible. Do you have anything for us?

"Sir, there was one incident yesterday," George explained. "Right after the morning chapel service, the generator malfunctioned. Maintenance reported that water leaked into the reserve tank and had some how gotten into the main fuel tank. That caused the engine to kick off. It has been really raining awfully hard."

"I guess the monsoon has set in, but that should not be a problem for the project," Colonel Murphy added. "We will be shipping the mock satellite on an aircraft capable of landing on your runway. It should arrive within the couple of days, so the mail will be on that plane with the satellite. I will advise you when it takes off so that you can prepare to unload it as quickly as possible."

"Sir, can you give me some idea of its weight?" George asked.

"I believe that it should weigh about 1,500 pounds," Murphy responded. "But it will be light enough to be launched in a geosynchronous orbit to an altitude of approximately about 22,200 miles."

"When the mechanism is attached, it will be tough to move because together, they will weigh about 3,000 pounds," George stated.

"That should be no problem because proper equipment will accompany the satellite and will stay with you until you can fly the finished product back to HQ," Murphy said. "George, do the best you can in the shortest time possible. I'll fax the drawings to you so that engineering can study them. Good luck, Captain. And please give your new wife our regards. Good day, Captain."

George walked down to the engineering office and met with Mr. James Crenshaw and informed him of the division commander's orders. Mr. Crenshaw did not seem to be one bit surprised that George had been ordered to be prepared for the incoming satellite.

"They will be faxing prints so that you can note any needed corrections made during assembly of the mechanisms," Captain Lee advised. "I will get the prints to you when I receive them, and I will let you know when to expect the delivery of the satellite. Have a good day, Mr. Crenshaw."

He left Crenshaw's office and looked for Laura. She was examining the weapon shielding.

George asked, "How does it look?"

"Actually, it looks pretty good," she answered. "In space, I doubt if shielding will be needed at all. It would shave hundreds of pounds of weight off the payload and make it less expensive to place into orbit."

"I will put your idea before the colonel and Mr. Crenshaw," George replied. "Good idea, honey. I just wanted to stop by and say I love you. See you at lunch."

She walked over to him and hugged and kissed him. "I love you too, you handsome dude."

From the engineering section, George headed for the science department where Dr. Charles Piton was busily perusing data recorded at the time of the weapon's test. He looked up, almost startled, as George told him, "Good morning."

"Oh my, Captain, you almost scared me," Piton said. "I was in such deep concentration."

"How do things look, Doctor?" George asked.

"Apparently, the shields did what they were designed to do," Piton replied.

"I just left engineering. While there, my wife, Laura suggested that maybe the shields would not be needed when the device is in orbit," George informed Dr. Piton.

"I don't see why that wouldn't work, sir," Piton replied. "In fact, that sounds practical and would save thousands of dollars per launch."

"May I tell my boss that you agree with the idea, Doctor?" George asked.

"You surely may, sir," Dr. Piton said with a smile. "You certainly have a smart lady and quite a good-looking one as well.

George left the science department and walked down to the security section to meet with Lt. Dewitt and inform him about the delivery of the satellite that would arrive Thursday evening by airplane. On his way, Harry met him.

"Walk with me to the Security Office, Harry." Harry followed him into the office where Lt. Dewitt was viewing security tapes.

"Captain, I'm sure glad to see you two guys," Dewitt said with a serious tone. "After the incident with the water-contaminated fuel tank, reviewing the tapes from the night before the blackout, we found that someone intentionally contaminated the water. It was not an accident that caused the fuel problem, sir."

"Well, I'll be a monkey's uncle," Harry said, shaking his head.

"Can you get a fix on the person responsible, Lieutenant?" George asked.

"I haven't yet, but I'm sure Sergeant Decker can help with this," the lieutenant responded. "He can clarify the fuzziest of pictures. I've seen him do it before, so it should be a breeze for him."

George told the lieutenant to keep him informed and then apprised him of the situation with the incoming flight containing the missile to be fitted with the mechanism and then fly it out. He told Harry and him to begin preparing for its arrival. George saw that it was lunchtime so he invited them to come to lunch with him. Both agreed, so they all headed for the cafeteria.

Laura entered as they were being seated. She got a tray of food and sat down beside George.

Back in the office, George passed on Laura's idea about eliminating the shielding for the mechanism. He also told that Dr Piton agreed that it would be a grand idea.

The remainder of the day was uneventful for which George was grateful. He spent a peaceful evening with his new bride.

## Day 15

As George entered his office, his secretary motioned to him that he had a call. He picked up the phone as he sat down behind his desk. "Captain Lee here."

"Captain Lee, this is Lt. Dewitt," returned the voice on the other end. "Sir, would you mind coming to my office? Sgt. Decker has clarified the video of the person who polluted the diesel fuel."

"I will be there right away, Lieutenant," George replied as he stood, placed the phone on the hook, and headed for the door.

He opened the door to Security and was greeted with broad smiles from Dewitt and Decker.

"Take a look at this, sir," Sgt. Decker said excitedly.

George could not believe the clarity of the picture. "Have you found his identity?"

Lt. Dewitt answered, "We have the computer scanning all our files for this guy, sir. It may take hours to finish the scan."

"I'm impressed. Once again, I say to you, good work, gentlemen," George told them. "Make sure security is beefed up around the perimeter just in case this guy decides to return. Let's get this picture distributed to all our troops. And I will let him know that you may need more men. Have Sgt. Decker show him this tape and then you three device some plan to catch this guy. We simply cannot afford to have him running free."

George thanked them and headed for his office to contact HQ.

The colonel picked up his phone. "Hello, George, I was just going to call you. What's up on your end?"

George answered, "Well, sir, since I last contacted you about the problem with the fuel contamination, Security has found the tape of a man pouring water into the fuel tank. We are running his picture through our personnel files to see if we can locate him as one of us."

"That figures!" Colonel Murphy practically yelled. "Our intelligence has intercepted a message to our enemies reporting the test firing of our mechanism. George, it looks serious. Apparently, they have found out somehow what we are doing on the island. As we speak, I am sending four antiaircraft units to be emplaced around the facility. Also, we are moving up the shipping time of the satellite so that it should arrive sometime later today. The fax of the prints is ready to be sent as soon as we are finished with our conversation. Please update Lt. Dewitt and First Sgt. Collins with this new information, and make sure that security is extra tight. This looks like war, George, and I'm afraid that you will need to send patrols to search for the culprit if he is not among your personnel. Try to take this man alive if possible. This is serious stuff we are dealing with. Probably as serious as stopping World War III. Keep me up-to-date, George"

"Roger on that, sir," George said. "I will do my best, sir."

George picked up the in-house phone and contacted Lt. Dewitt, Sgt. Decker, and Sgt. Collins to meet with him in his office ASAP. Within five minutes, all three were sitting around his desk.

"Gentlemen, the fuel incident has caused things to take a serious turn," George began. "I have just talked with HQ, and I was informed that the enemy knows what we are doing here on the island. A message was intercepted by our intelligence that reported our test firing to them. Lieutenant, have you found the suspect among our personnel?"

Sgt. Decker spoke up, "Excuse me, sir. May I answer that question, sir? There were no matches in our personnel files. That must mean that someone has infiltrated our island, and it wasn't one of our people."

"Yes, that is exactly why I called you together in this office. Antiaircraft guns are being sent and will be emplaced around our facility. We are to have patrols out searching for this man and if possible capture him alive. Gentlemen, it's critical that we get this done ASAP. We will pray that God will speed you along on your efforts and give you safety."

They all, in turn, excused themselves, and as they were leaving, George stopped Harry, "Hold up, Harry. May I talk to you a second?"

Harry stopped and turned back to George's desk. "What can I do for you, George?"

"Harry, with this latest turn of events, I'm really concerned about the failure of this mission," George confessed. "I don't want to say anything to Laura, but I feel as though you are the only one I can confide in who will not spread it all over God's creation. What do you think I should do?"

"George, I don't think you are failing at all," Harry replied. "No one I know could be doing a better job than you have done, sir. So don't be discouraged. I have the highest regards for you and your abilities, Captain. With God's help, you can get this thing done. Trust me, I've seen far less capable officers accomplish things by perseverance."

"Thanks, Harry, I really needed that bit of encouragement and that little push," George said, smiling. "I will try not to fail your confidence. Let me know when you come up with ideas about how to trap this guy. Thanks, Harry. I really mean it from the bottom of my heart. Now let's catch this guy."

They shook hands and George gave Harry a light hug and a pat on the back before they left the room. They walked toward the cafeteria. Laura met them at the door, so they entered together. After they entered, Sgt. Decker motioned for Harry to come over to his table. Harry excused himself and left Laura and George and went over to set by Decker. George heard Decker ask Harry to talk over plans on patrolling the area around the facility.

Laura and George enjoyed a quiet lunch in the corner of the cafeteria. Sgt. Grant ambled over to their table and placed a bit of cake and ice cream in front of them. "Captain, I know that you are under a great deal of stress, so here is a little something to cheer you and the missus up. It's on the house." He laughed a deep laugh as he walked away.

"Hey, Sergeant," George said in time to catch him before he got away, "do you happen to sing bass?"

"Why, yes I do," Grant answered. "Before I joined up, I sang in a professional southern gospel group."

"Wow! I'll keep that in mind," George commented. "I've been thinking about forming a singing group for chapel services. I'll talk with Chaplain Clapp and see if he can get three others to help."

"Hey, that would be great," Grant said happily. "I can't tell you how much I've missed singing."

Laura stood and went over to the sergeant and said, "Would you mind singing in a mixed quartet? I can sing lead and harmonize a bit. Perhaps one of my friends could sing alto or tenor. If it doesn't work, we've lost nothing, but a practice."

Grant agreed, "I'm sure we can find someone to sing baritone. I heard Sgt. Decker singing in church the other day. Maybe we could get him to sing with us. I'll ask him before he leaves today." He left Laura and headed toward the table where Sergeants Decker and Collins were sitting.

Both Laura and George were excited about the prospect of a quartet being formed. George interrupted the hilarity by standing. "Meanwhile, I've got work that requires my attention."

When George headed back to his office, he was glad for the positive distraction that forming the quartet had given. In about an hour, Harry knocked on the door and, when he entered, reported that he had dispatched two six-member squads to scour the area to search for the saboteur. Both squads returned without finding the man or any evidence of his existence.

Two more squads were to expand the search perimeters. Night was falling so these squads were equipped with night vision equipment. The man would surely have left some trace of his ventures around the island.

Just before they left, George got a call from HQ telling him that they had identified the intruder as Amos Farrago, a mercenary soldier who hired out to anyone willing to pay for his services. Amos Farrago was a dangerous man, an expert in weapons and hand-to-hand combat techniques with a black belt in marshal arts. The captain advised the squads, "Gentlemen, this man is very dangerous, and according to my information, he kills without mercy. Please do not become cocky and think that he will not be a problem because I guarantee that he is and will be if you let your guard down for a millisecond. I suspect that he will not give up without a fight. When he is apprehended, keep him in shackles, and do not take your eyes off him. He has escaped from confinement and left bodies lying about. He is a lethal adversary and will not be taken into custody easily. Please do not take any chances with him. Also, keep in mind that he may not be working alone. We would like for him to be captured alive, but the most important thing is that you all return in one piece. Good luck, gentlemen."

Both squads checked their radios, their night vision equipment, weapons, and with solemn and determined looks, exited the facility. They were instructed to report in every hour on the hour. George instructed the sergeant of the guard to call him no matter the hour if they encountered the intruder, any sign of him, or if anything unusual happened anywhere near the facility. Monitors were to be watched round the clock for the slightest deviation from the normal pattern of things. Nothing was to be considered unimportant.

He called Sgt. Grant and arranged to have dinner for Laura and himself to be sent to his quarters. Laura and he would hopefully have a few minutes to spend alone before any trouble was reported.

# The Capture

## Day 16

After a relaxing meal, they decided to take a nap. They were both fast asleep; the phone rang. To George, it sounded as though the ringing was part of his dream. In it, he was asleep back home in the upstairs bedroom when he heard the home phone ringing downstairs and heard his mother answer it. That's when he became aware of Laura's voice telling the sergeant that he would be right there.

"George, honey," Laura said, "I'm sorry, but the sergeant of the guard just called to let you know that you needed to come to his office immediately."

He looked over at his watch. "0300 hours. It's about the time that I thought we would have something."

He was happy that they had a cup of coffee waiting for him at the guard room. He took a sip.

"Good coffee. What's up, Sergeant?"

Sgt. Hitter replied, "Thanks. We have just had a report that they have found a campsite. Most likely it is Amos Farrago's. They are awaiting instructions."

Captain Lee requested the radio, then pressed the call button, "Alligator 20 to Alligator 23, over!"

His radio squelched then. "Alligator 23, Alligator 21, go ahead. We have breakfast on the table. We are awaiting instructions, over."

George replied, "Alligator 23, please take positions around the table and await the special guest to arrive. Wait until he is seated unless you hear him saying grace. If he says grace, join him for dinner ASAP, Alligator 21, over."

"Roger, 23, out.

Sgt. Hitter took the radio and called the other two squads and advised them that the campsite had been located by the second squad and that they were to rendezvous with the second squad at their location. He advised them to proceed and approach with caution.

The first squad responded, "Alligator 22, roger, wilco, out."

Then, the third squad reported in "Alligator 24, roger, wilco, out."

They waited in anxious silence as suspense built for a couple hours. The silence was finally broken. "Alligator two-zero this is Alligator 23, over."

Sgt. Hitter pressed the button. "23, this is 20, over."

The first squad radioed, "20, the guest has just arrived, but does not seem to be saying grace, over."

The second squad then broke in, "Alligator 20, this is Alligator 23, over."

"Go ahead, 23," the sergeant replied.

"23, approaching 22's position," the second squad announced.

About that time, George heard gunfire. Sgt. Hitter frantically pressed the send key requesting reports from either squad.

"22, report; 23, report; 24, report."

Finally, the first squad reported, "22 to 20, we have seated the dinner guest and have sustained zero casualties, over."

"22, this is 21, please escort your dinner guest to the main banquet table in the mansion," Captain Lee instructed. "Good news and great job, men. All Alligator units, 20 out."

"22, roger, wilco, out," came back the reply.

"Sgt. Hitter," Captain Lee instructed, "please inform First Lt. Dewitt to meet me at the security office."

Sgt. Hitter stood, saluted, and replied, "Yes, sir," and quickly left the room. There was a PFC manning the radio as George left the guard room and headed toward the security office.

It took the squads about thirty minutes to return to the facility. Captain Lee was waiting at the door when the squad leaders entered with the prisoner.

"Well, if it isn't Amos Farrago, the fuel and water pollution man."

Farrago snarled, "Hey, Captain Lee. I've heard a lot about you and your family."

"Lt. Dewitt, please take the prisoner to his room," George instructed. "I'll get Sgt. Collins to visit with our obnoxious visitor."

George headed straight to his office and contacted the colonel's office. Some duty sergeant answered the phone.

George instructed him, "Please wake the colonel and get him to the phone. Have him call me when he arrives. Tell him it's an emergency."

It took approximately forty-five minutes before the phone rang.

"Hello, Colonel," George answered anxiously.

"What's the emergency, George?" Colonel Murphy asked sleepily.

"Number 1," George answered, "We have captured Amos Farrago. Number 2, when I first addressed him, he said that he had heard a lot about me and my family. I think my family may be in danger, Colonel."

"I'll get someone on it right away," Murphy advised, then asked, "Has the plane arrived yet?"

"No, sir," George answered. "Wait, I hear the runway camouflage moving, so it must be arriving as we speak, sir. Please protect my family. Let me know what happens with them, sir, I'd really appreciate it."

"I'll take care of everything, George," Murphy advised, "and please try not to worry about them. I'll get back with you when I learn anything. Right now, you have enough to concern you on the island."

George went and awakened Sgt. Collins. "Sorry, Harry, we have a couple things happening. At this moment, an airplane is delivering the satellite. Guess what else, Harry."

Harry looked puzzled, and then answered, "You got him!"

George was surprised. "We have him in security now."

"Wow, you have been a busy man, sir," Harry said in a jovial tone. "Where do you want me first, sir?"

"Bring your specialty tools and come with me to the holding cell where the prisoner is being held," George advised Harry. Harry grabbed a small packet from the closet and followed the captain out the door.

They arrived at the security office and were greeted by Sgt. Decker, "Well, a happy good morning, gentlemen, our guest is awaiting your arrival."

George answered, "Have you searched him?"

"He has been stripped, cavity searched, and given prisoner clothing, sir," Sgt. Decker replied.

"Great," George thanked Sgt. Decker for the information and asked about Lt. Dewitt's location.

"Lt. Dewitt went to supervise the unloading of the satellite, sir," Sgt. Decker reported as he stood and led the way to Amos Farrago's cell. Farrago was lying on the bunk when they arrived. He had been asleep, but when he heard them approaching, he stood to his feet.

Sgt. Collins yelled, "Sit down, Farrago!"

Farrago hesitated, and Sgt. Collins pushed him back down on the bunk.

"Sergeant, it's a good thing my hands are cuffed or I would pound you into the ground like a worm," Farrago seethed.

Captain Lee stopped him. "Save the theatrics for later. Right now, you are going to answer a few questions for us."

The captain had Decker bring a stool for Farrago. Decker and Collins grabbed Farrago and forced him over to the stool. Harry took a couple plastic wire ties from out of the inside of his cap. He also pulled some long sharp pins from his collar. As Captain Lee and Sgt. Decker held Farrago, Sgt. Collins strapped his ankles to the stool legs. He then fastened wire ties from the cuffs behind Farrago's back to the rung on his stool. As Sgt. Collins stood and started to walk away, he caught his foot on one of the stool legs and Farrago fell to one side on to the concrete floor.

"Oh, how clumsy of me. I'll try not to be so clumsy if you try not to be an inconsiderate and uncooperative jerk. Do you get my meaning, Farrago? Now why don't you tell us what you meant by telling Captain Lee that you know all about him and his family?"

Farrago pursed his lips. Sgt. Collins pulled the long sharp pins from where he had placed them after he had moved behind the prisoner.

"Really, I hate to begin our relationship in such a painful manner, but we need that information from the only source available, you."

Quick as a flash, Collins jabbed the pins deep into the nape of Farrago's neck. His immediate reaction was a smirk. The smirk was replaced immediately with a grimace and scream that would have resounded a city block in New York City. He struggled to get up and fell flat on his side again. He lay there writhing in pain, trying to say something. Harry reached down and pulled the pins from his neck.

He actually thanked Harry. "Thanks, you really are good. I know that you will break me eventually so I will tell you all I know."

Harry instructed, "Don't try this type of delay tactic on me, Farrago. I have seen them all while I was over in Iraq and Afghanistan and have learned a lot about how prisoners try to avoid direct answers." Harry held the pins as though he was contemplating whether or not to wait or administer them directly.

"Okay," Farrago yelled, "I work for a consortium of Eastern Nations that, as you already know, have built a weapon so powerful it may destroy a major portions of our nation's cities and plunge us into World War III. I really didn't know that when I hired on with them. I really don't want that to happen."

"So believe me, I just gave them enough information to let them think I had everything under control here. I didn't think you would discover me quite so quickly. I planned to make some kind of explosion some distance from the facility to fool them into thinking I had destroyed it. I told them that it would occur tomorrow...this evening about 1100 hours. So they will be watching for the explosion. You will find the explosives about a thousand yards from my campsite. If you want to fool them, you will need to set off that explosion. Please listen. As sure as there is a God in heaven, I am telling you truth. As you know, I'm not a goody-two-shoe, but I do not want my country to be annihilated."

Captain Lee motioned for Sgt. Collins to cut the ties. He then removed the handcuffs and directed Farrago to take a seat on the bunk.

"Thanks for your answers, Farrago," Captain Lee said. "Now please tell me what you meant by the remark about my family."

Farrago answered, "Captain, I'm sorry, but if they find out that I am captured, your family will be in grave danger. Please let me radio them and pretend that everything is going as planned. I am scheduled to report in about forty-five minutes."

George ran down the hall and grabbed the phone to HQ. "Colonel, Murphy, if they find out that we have captured Farrago, they will kill my family. Also, he is supposed to give them an update in about thirty-five minutes. He promised that he will tell them that all is going according to schedule. Should we let him make contact, sir?"

Colonel Murphy responded, "Use your own judgment, George. It just may stop WWIII, son. Take care of things as you see fit. If Farrago is cooperative, give him the benefit of the doubt. It just might save millions of lives."

George ran back to security. He burst through the door and yelled, "Farrago must make the scheduled contact time with his leaders. Quickly, let's get him to a radio."

George asked if there was any way there could be a five-second delay before the transmission was sent. Sergeant Decker began searching in another room and returned quickly with a device that he said would delay the messages five seconds.

Farrago hurried to the radio and dialed in the frequency, pressed the call button, gave the code word, and reported in Korean, "A-F to King Kong, everything is going as planned, over."

There was a sound like the hissing of an upset cat warning something to keep away, *skurrrr*, then a voice, "King Kong to AF, that's good news. We are awaiting the fireworks tonight. King Kong, out."

Captain Lee addressed Farrago, "It looks as though you may not be all bad, I suppose. I thank you for doing that."

Farrago replied, "Captain Lee, I have family that may die if my employers are not stopped, and I simply do not want that to happen. I really wish you the best of luck, and I will cooperate in any way I can, sir."

"Thanks for your offer," Captain Lee said sincerely. "Now let's get the explosives set for their show this evening, Farrago. Where do we need to go?" He turned to Sgt. Collins. "Sgt. Collins, assemble a crew of your best men and let's go along with Farrago to set the explosives and assist him in the preparation of the 'fireworks' for our waiting spectators." Then he instructed Sgt. Decker, "Contact Lt. Dewitt and pass along this order, 'get everyone out of bed, the scientists, engineers, and erection crews, and get them started working on mating the satellite and the mechanism. Get it ready for shipping ASAP.' If there are any developments, I will be out with Sgt. Collins overseeing the setting of the explosives. I can be contacted by radio as 'Alligator 21.'"

Sgt. Decker saluted. "Yes, sir. I wish you and your men the best of luck, Captain Lee."

"Thanks, Sgt. Decker," George said. "It is important that Lt. Dewitt is brought up to speed and reminded just how important it is that we finish this project before the enemy realizes what has gone down here."

Sgt. Collins returned with a squad of seven men. "We are ready, sir."

Farrago stood and walked over to Sgt. Collins and waited at the door. George followed behind the squad while Sgt. Collins acted as point. Farrago was third in the column, and two men with weapons at the ready walked a couple feet behind him and on either side. They cautiously approached Farrago's campsite. Farrago told Collins that there were radio-activated explosives hidden in his tent. Sure enough, a search in the location revealed that it was exactly where he had told Collins it was.

"Anything else we need?" Collins asked.

Farrago answered, "There is nothing more here, but you had better let me lead from here on to the explosives stash because I have booby traps set up at several locations around the cache of explosives."

Captain Lee nodded in agreement, so Sgt. Collins allowed Farrago to take the point.

The two soldiers who were guarding Farrago stayed close to him as they moved farther toward the cache site. George motioned for Harry to wait on him. "Harry, I don't think Farrago wanted to do damage to our facility. What's your opinion?"

Harry agreed, "Yes, but I'm not yet completely convinced. He acts like he really wants to help. Let's wait and see until after the explosion tonight before we decide what action to take. I think I know what you have in mind, sir."

"If and when you agree," George acquiesced, "call him Far-to-go, and it will happen, but we must have it occur away from our compound."

Farrago pointed out several hidden booby traps located along the path. As they arrived, he advised Sgt. Collins that there were claymores situated around the area. The group waited while he went about disarming them, much to the relief of his squad. They had seen the damage that these types of mines could inflict. Finally, Farrago gave the "all clear." Farrago told the captain the approximate time the enemy's satellite would pass over the area. "They will want to see the explosions so that will be the best time to begin the fireworks, sir. About a quarter of a mile due east and a bit closer to the facility are some abandoned buildings. These would make it look more realistic if they were used in the presentation. We can make it look like the facility is completely demolished."

## Sound the Alarm

Captain Lee agreed with Farrago's suggestion, so he radioed an order for Sgt. Decker, "Bring about twenty-five more men to help carry and rig up explosives in abandoned structures."

It took about forty minutes for Decker to arrive with his troops. Farrago began to instruct Collins's men where to place the explosives. They were set in locations that would approximate the size of the facility. George hoped the explosions would actually fool anyone watching from satellite. Things went along well with Farrago directing the placement of the C-4 charges. Receiving devices were attached to enough explosives to demolish the structures and many of the larger trees.

It took about four and a half hours to finalize the preparations. Sgt. Collins approached Captain Lee.

"Captain, we are almost ready, and it appears that Far-to-go has given us the break that only his cooperation could have enabled."

George smiled. "I totally agree. Let's walk over to the side of that far building where no one can read our lips or listen in."

They talked about plans for the explosions as they meandered over to the place where George had indicated. When they stopped, George asked, "Harry, do you have any suggestions about how to accomplish this?"

"Well, during the explosions, there will be a lot of excitement, and our people will be distracted. During that time, we should be able to get him out of sight," Harry advised. Almost as an afterthought, he added, "Sir, you do realize that you are going to take a lot of flack over this, don't you?"

"I'm sure I will, but HQ knows that Farrago is a tough guy, so I don't think it will be too difficult for us to explain. And I will make sure that he leaves me lying on the ground with at least a black eye. I don't think he will have any problem with giving me one after our treatment in security, do you?" Harry agreed with George.

Captain Lee left guards equipped with radios and night vision equipment posted around the area. He warned that if they failed the world as they knew it may no longer exist.

George and Harry walked with Farrago and his two guards. While Sgt. Collins distracted the guards with conversation about their military experience, family, or any other topic that would keep their attention off Farrago, the captain walked to within whispering distance of Farrago and motioned for him to keep quiet and not react.

He yelled, "You coward, what kind of man are you?" Then in a whisper, he asked, "Do you have the means to get off the island if you just happened to escape? Just nod if you do."

Farrago nodded, and then looked angry.

George continued, "Good! All right, here's the plan. When the explosions begin, there should be a lot of distraction. I will try to have you off to the side, somewhere close to cover so that you should be able to easily get away without being seen. As you leave, I want you to knock me out and then hightail it off this island ASAP." Then in a louder tone, "You traitor, I ought to tie you up and leave you to die in one of these buildings."

Farrago mouthed, "Thank you, and God bless you for this. It will not go unrewarded, Captain."

George whispered, "Thanks for all your help." Once again louder, "I ought to kill you myself." He punched Farrago a glancing blow on the chin, knocking him down. As Farrago lay there, he winked at George and nodded.

Farrago yelled, "We will see who dies, you white swine!"

The guards rushed up and grabbed Farrago, who struggled with them a bit, then calmed down as George walked over to Collins.

"Good job, Captain," Harry said quietly. "I was almost convinced you were about to kill him, and I knew what was happening."

"Great! I think it will work out for the best." George smiled, rubbing his fist. "Man! He sure is one tough hombre. That punch didn't even faze him." Then he changed the subject, "Okay, make sure our guards stay hidden. They should be relieved every two hours so that they will be fresh. When we get back to the compound, we should get some rest too."

After everything was set, they headed back to the compound. George looked up Laura and explained their plans and then they headed back to their quarters to get some shut eye.

Some time later, George jerked awake, washed and shaved, brushed his teeth, and then headed for the office. He reported to HQ what had transpired and the plans that were in place, "And, Colonel Murphy, we are about ready to ship the satellite with the device attached."

Colonel Murphy sounded ecstatic. "Captain Lee, you have been a very busy man. I will have a plane ready to go when you give us the word."

George replied, "Sir, I'm not sure that is the best idea. Perhaps we had better ship it by boat under the cover of darkness because the enemy should be convinced after the fireworks tonight that this facility has been annihilated.

Murphy sounded worried now. "George, that would almost be impossible. Perhaps the plane could land one evening, be loaded during the next day, then take off by cover of night again. Let me get back with you on this."

George headed for the erection area where they were working to mount the device up to the satellite. He was actually amazed that they were bolting it together. James Crenshaw walked over with a Cheshire cat smile.

"Captain, by God's grace, we've got it done. It should be ready to ship within the hour."

George grabbed Crenshaw and gave him a big hug. "Man! You have just made my day, James Crenshaw." They both jumped around a bit, but then realized how juvenile they must have appeared to others and stopped.

Laura walked over and gave George a hug. "I see you got your nap out. I was about to come get you up, but you showed up just in time."

Crenshaw interrupted, "Hey, Captain, I heard you captured some island intruder, is that true?"

"Yes," George began, "when we had that blackout because of the generator, someone had purposely contaminated the fuel. We found the culprit and took him into custody. He has actually been very cooperative. I'd like to chit-chat a bit longer, but I had better get on the horn with HQ again and give them this good news. Great job you and your crews have done, Crenshaw. I'll get back with you in a short while."

George went to security to check on how things were going at the fireworks site and found that everything was proceeding without incident. He also checked on Farrago, who seemed to be doing all right.

Farrago smiled at the sight of George. "Captain, for a Christian, you have a pretty good punch."

George asked, "Are you being treated well?"

Still smiling, Farrago nodded. "What do you think? Just wait until I get you alone, you will pay for treating me like this!"

George returned the smile. "You had better watch your tongue. Do you know what I think? I think you will get to see the fireworks display that our enemies were so eager for you to use this facility. Then your friends will be seeking revenge on you, my angry friend!"

Farrago turned away from the camera and mouthed the words, "God bless you. You will be repaid with His blessings." Then he screamed, "Get out of here! You are without mercy, and I will pay you back for this!"

George nodded to the guard to close the cell door, and as he left, he yelled back at Farrago, "I will see to it that you get what's coming to you, you sneaky coward!"

On his way out, George instructed Lt. Dewitt to have Farrago escorted by Sgt. Collins to the demolition at about 0215 hours. The lieutenant looked surprised at first. "Sir, I know that you have a problem with the prisoner, but do you think that is a wise decision?"

"I think Sgt. Collins is quite capable of controlling the prisoner, and I would like for him to watch the failure of his plan to destroy this facility. Don't you think that would be a bit of poetic justice, Lieutenant?"

"I suppose so, Captain," Dewitt replied with a look of doubt. "How about sending a couple guards to assist Sgt. Collins, just in case something goes wrong?"

"If you think that is warranted, Lieutenant," George agreed. "We will see you this evening."

Back in the office, he got a call from Col. Murphy. "Hello, this is Captain Lee."

"George, this is Col. Murphy. We have decided to send a Boeing CH-47 Chinook chopper from a carrier located about seventy-five miles from the island to pick up your article," Murphy began.

"Colonel, the device is ready to ship," George reported. "They were finishing mating them within the last thirty minutes. It hasn't been confirmed yet, but unless something has changed, it should be ready to pick up. We are planning to have the fireworks about 0-300 hours, tomorrow morning, just as the enemy's satellite is passing over. So, sir, in my opinion, the pickup should be made by 0-400 hrs or some time after the explosions just before dawn."

"It would be great if the parcel was ready to ship by 0-430 hrs. We will proceed at that time. Be careful with all that ordinance, I'm sure we will see the fireworks, but I would like to have the project completed before then so no further activity is required on the island. That would trick the enemy into believing their plan has actually worked. I'm excited, so let's make this happen, Captain."

Murphy hung up without saying good-bye. George wasn't surprised because he knew that the colonel was overwhelmed with excitement and relief.

George contacted Mr. Crenshaw and advised him to have the assembled unit ready to ship by 0400 hours. Mr. Crenshaw was excited as the colonel. "I think this is about over. God certainly has been with us. I believe tomorrow morning we should have a praise meeting to celebrate our successes with this project."

George was way too tense to sleep despite the fact that he was dead tired.

## Day 17

Just before 0100 hours, Sgt. Collins knocked on George's door. Laura had gone to bed and was sleeping soundly. George walked with Sgt. Collins who reported that his men and Farrago were ready to start for the fireworks site.

Harry said, "Sir, we will have to be discreet with Farrago to pull this thing off."

George nodded. "We will both keep watch to make sure that no one is looking when the time comes."

They walked into the room where the troops were waiting.

"Attention," someone yelled.

Everyone snapped to attention, even Farrago.

"At ease, gentlemen," Captain Lee ordered. "Gentlemen, soon, we should be getting off this island. What we do tonight is dangerous, so be extra careful because the result will influence the futures of our families and may prevent WWIII. Now let's go make some fireworks, what do you say?"

Everyone cheered at the captain's statements.

"Sergeants, move your men out," George ordered. Lt. Dewitt was to remain with Farrago as ordered by Captain Lee. He would follow in about thirty-five minutes.

"Yes, sir," the sergeants responded. "Squads, move out." They exited the building in an orderly fashion. They spaced themselves approximately fifteen feet apart as they left the shelter of a porch in an effort to conceal their numbers from possible prying eyes of an unseen enemy.

Approximately an hour and fifteen minutes later, they arrived at the site. George had everything checked one final time before the demolition was due to begin. There were only whispered orders or hand signals directing the troops as they disbursed among the structures. Everyone was instructed to use the buddy system to prevent someone from accidently being left in a building during the fireworks. They erected camouflaged protection a safe distance from the site. The fastest runner among the men was selected to stay within the required signal range to activate the devices.

He should be able to get back to protection before the fireworks began. Lt. Dewitt and two guards arrived with Farrago in handcuffs. They waited near a clump of shaggy bushes. Captain gave the runner the activation device, and he sprinted off to await the prearranged signal to activate the explosives. There was a seven-minute delay so the runner should easily make the quarter mile back before the fireworks began. Everyone, including Lt. Dewitt, was anxiously awaiting the runner's return. He handcuffed Farrago's hands behind his back around a small tree and went to a better vantage point. Harry saw his chance and sauntered over close to Farrago.

George watched as Harry removed something from his blouse pocket and placed it in Farrago's hand. Everyone became quiet as the runner raced across a small clearing in front of their position. After he arrived, there was a delay of about two minutes, and suddenly, the night was ablaze with orange, yellow, and red flames as the C-4 did its damage.

Someone yelled, "Just think, that could have been us. Thank God, we caught the intruder. Finally, the explosions subsided, and only the flames of a burning jungle persisted. Captain Lee motioned for the sergeants to lead their men back to the compound. They silently began moving their men back to the facility where they knew hot coffee would be available at the cafeteria. Suddenly, out of the darkness, Lt. Dewitt came running toward Captain Lee and Sgt Collins.

"Captain," he whispered breathlessly, "Farrago has escaped."

George acted surprised. "Where was he? And where were you?"

Lt. Dewitt led them toward the tree where he had left Farrago. "Sir, I don't understand how he could have possibly escaped. I had him handcuffed with his arms behind him around this tree. The guards were with me watching the fireworks."

"Well," Sgt. Collins whispered, "here are handcuffs, but Farrago is nowhere in sight. Let me get some of the men and make a search."

Captain Lee said, "Hold up, Sergeant, it's too dangerous to try that tonight. I don't know if we should expose ourselves tonight. We have to just let him go because we need to load up and leave soon. And we don't want to let the enemy know that any of us are alive. I'll contact HQ for advice."

Lt. Dewitt looked worried. "Sir, I am responsible for his escape. I deserve some sort of punishment. You should place those handcuffs on me for my dereliction of duty, sir."

"We'll talk more about that later," George encouraged. "Right now, let's get back to base and get some breakfast before we leave. I suppose that the enemy is rejoicing about now. Don't worry, Lieutenant, I'll take care of you, son. Now take it easy, and keep all this under your hat. Don't even mention it to Sgt. Decker. Okay?"

"Yes, sir," Lt. Dewitt said with a sigh of relief.

Back at the facility, all the troops were thanked for their great efforts and success of the fireworks.

"We pray that it has fooled our enemies into thinking that the facility has been destroyed. Get some breakfast and prepare for the exodus."

That news was met with cheers.

"As soon as we get the satellite loaded up, we will be getting off this island and headed for the mainland."

There was more cheering.

"Lt. Dewitt, do you have anything?"

Dewitt shook his head.

"How about you sergeants, do you have any questions or comments?"

They also shook their heads in the negative.

Captain Lee gave the command, "Get some chow and get ready to go. You are dismissed!" Once again, cheers rang out as the men and women dispersed. The officers and noncoms walked together discussing the events of the morning and considered how long HQ might take to get them off the island. Before they separated, Captain Lee pulled Lt. Dewitt aside and reminded him that he should not worry and that he would take care of the situation. Lt. Dewitt indicated that he was heart sick and remorseful about the whole matter and did not expect any preferential treatment.

George headed to his quarters and found Laura getting dressed.

"Hi, honey, where have you been?" she asked. "When I woke up, you were gone."

George smiled. "We went off and set of a bunch of explosions to make the enemy think that this facility is destroyed. We will be getting out of here pretty quickly. Let's have some breakfast and get ready to leave."

"Oh, honey, that would be great," she said with a big smile. "Then we can have some semblance of a normal marriage."

"I'm looking forward to it," George said as he walked over and took her in his arms, "but it hasn't been too awful here, has it?"

Her answer was smothered by a lingering kiss.

Laura and he talked until just before 0400 hours when he heard the unique sound of the Chinook's chopper blades. No lights lit up the runway and there were no lights flashing on the chopper as it landed. There was however a soldier with flashlights guiding the landing. Timed perfectly with the landing, the satellite was pushed to where it could be lifted by the Chinook. Within fifteen minutes, the Chinook lifted off with its precious cargo. It had taken many man hours and thousands of dollars to achieve this historic moment.

George and Laura quickly finished breakfast. Everyone was excited, and the atmosphere was cheerful tense now that the mission was accomplished.

James Crenshaw walked over to George and said, "Sir, it has been a great pleasure serving our great country under your watchful eye." Then he turned toward Laura, "And you, young lady, I'm so glad that I had the pleasure of working with you. I feel that you have a great future and will be a very successful engineer. I would be willing to work with you on any project. I think your life with this man will be truly blessed."

"It's been great so far," Laura said with a gleam in her eyes, "and I expect it will be even better if and when we achieve life above ground, instead of underground like the way we have lived thus far."

They chatted for a bit longer, but were interrupted by Laura's friends who wished her the best. George excused himself and headed for the office. He contacted HQ and arranged for the colonel to contact him. Promptly at 0415 hours, the red phone rang.

"Good morning, Captain Lee speaking," George answered.

"Good morning, Captain Lee, this is Colonel Murphy," the voice that George had come to recognize said. "Once again, you are to be congratulated. It looks as though you have pulled it off. Our intelligence reports that the enemy is elated because they destroyed the island facility. You should hear choppers approaching any time now. Everyone will be air lifted to a ship near you."

"Sir," George interrupted, "I have some bad news, Farrago escaped. He was actually handcuffed with his arms around a tree. Somehow, he was able to remove his handcuffs and escape. He is a very talented man, sir."

Murphy said, "Oh no. That's bad news, who is responsible?"

George answered cautiously, "I reckon that would be me, sir. The buck stops here, you know. Let me give you some information about him that you may not realize. Farrago has family living in the USA that he expected they would be killed if the enemy's attack was successful, so he led us to the cache of explosives and then helped us set them up. Sir, I think he probably could have escaped earlier if he had chosen, but he felt the explosions would confuse our enemies and perhaps our success would save his family."

"Thanks for that," Murphy said with a hint of understanding, "perhaps this should remain top-top secret, if you know what I mean. About your choppers, they will arrive at fifteen minutes intervals until everybody is off the island. Send the civilians first, and then the military personnel. On that first chopper, there will be enough explosives to destroy the facility. After everyone has been evacuated, use as many people as you need to destroy the entire facility. Set the time so that you will have enough time to get on the chopper and fly a sufficient distance to avoid damage to the chopper. Understand?"

"Yes, Sir Colonel Murphy," George replied, "I hope to see you real soon, sir."

As soon as he hung up the phone, George called Security and talked with Lt. Dewitt. When he came on the phone, George laughed.

"I told you I would take care of the Farrago situation. Congratulations, you are free from any action on that. According to Colonel Murphy, anything about Farrago is considered top-top secret. It is never to be discussed with anyone from here on out—nobody. What I need now, Lieutenant, is that you get everyone into the dining room ASAP so we can begin getting out of here."

Lt. Dewitt replied, "Yes, sir, and thank you, Captain."

Soon, Lt Dewitt announced over the intercom, "May I have your attention please? All personnel are requested to report to the dining room ASAP. Thank you."

The announcement was repeated three times at five-minute intervals.

Everyone gathered in the cafeteria. Lt. Dewitt called for attention when Captain Lee arrived. All military snapped to attention.

"At ease, ladies and gentlemen!" George ordered and then continued, "As you all probably know, our mission here is completed. You probably heard the choppers arriving. They are here to transport us off this island beginning as soon as we are ready. We will leave in groups of forty-five, with civilian personnel evacuated first. Please take only the minimal baggage necessary. Let me remind all of you that everything that has transpired during your stay here is as

Colonel Murphy told me on the phone a few minutes ago, top-top secret. For now, all incidents stay on this island and are not to be in any way discussed with anyone, not even among those who are here. Perhaps later in life, you will be allowed to do so, but for now, zip it. You all signed a secrecy agreement before being assigned to this mission, so I think you know the importance of that document. Any violation of that agreement will be considered an act of treason against the sovereign nation of the United States of America. What we have accomplished here may in fact become a factor in preventing WW III. Before all you civilians are excused, I may not have the opportunity to meet with you again, so let me tell you that it has been a pleasure to meet you and to work alongside you. May God bless each of you and prosper your future. Get your things and meet at the flight area in twenty minutes. Department heads are responsible to assure that all your personnel are accounted for before you board a chopper. When your people have all boarded, report that to Lt. Dewitt, then you may board. Listen up, everyone. You do not want to be here when this place explodes. All military personnel will meet near the runways inside this compound at the end of this meeting. God bless you all. Thanks again for your dedication and a job well done."

They cheered and then left quickly and silently.

After the civilian personnel exited the cafeteria, George instructed the military personnel, "I need a few volunteers to assist me in setting explosives throughout this facility. That will hopefully complete the ruse of this morning's explosions. We will be on the last chopper after we set the charges. Could I see a show of hands of those who will volunteer for this final duty on this project? Lt. Dewitt, would you go over to the far corner and assist me with this?"

Dewitt yelled, "Yes, sir." He then stood and moved toward the far corner.

George continued, "You volunteers, please follow Lt. Dewitt, and wait. The rest of you are released to your NCOs."

The remaining soldiers moved to where their sergeants were waiting and George headed over to the waiting volunteers. He walked up to Lt. Dewitt and shook his hand. He asked the two NCOs that had volunteered to come forward. As they approached his position, he shook their hands and addressed them by name, "Platoon Sergeant Thomas Decker, First Sergeant Harry Collins," and turning toward Lt. Dewitt, he continued, "and First Lieutenant Patrick Dewitt, your expertise has been of indispensable assistance in solving of the fuel contamination and capturing the spy responsible for it. You have my most sincere thanks." He turned to the remainder of the volunteers. "Your dedication to service has been a boon to the success of our mission. The three men standing before you will supervise the unloading and placement of the charges we will receive on the first evacuation chopper. We will have approximately fifty minutes to get these explosives dispersed, set, and armed. When that last copter lands, we must have everything ready and be ready to board. After we are at a safe distance, I will remotely activate the charges from the helicopter. Some, if not all of you, assisted with the fireworks earlier. Things should proceed in a similar manner. We must be in a chopper, so it is important that everything goes smoothly for that to happen. Are there any questions?" There were no questions, so George turned to the lieutenant, "Lt. Dewitt, let's get that chopper unloaded."

As he turned to leave, Lt. Dewitt commanded, "Attention."

Everyone stood and stood at attention. As George moved away from the group, he motioned for Harry to meet him.

Lt. Dewitt ordered, "At ease. Now here is how we will proceed." His voice faded as George talked with Harry. "Harry, I think that everything is all right with the Farrago situation, but we shouldn't take any chances. At every opportunity, remind personnel they are not to discuss anything that transpired here. How are you doing? Are you ready to get back to Pam and Tommy?"

"It's been a lot less time here than I expected, but yes, I am happy at the thought of getting back to them," Harry answered. "I'm happy that you two newlyweds can get started on the outside world. You will get to meet the other one's parents. Won't that be great, George?"

"Actually," George shook his head, "I don't know. I'm a bit nervous about that. Laura's family wanted her to have a big formal wedding. But I guess I will face that when it arises. Well, I guess you had better join the others. I will meet you at the copter."

Harry nodded, saluted, did an about-face, and headed over to rejoin the group.

Laura had waited outside the cafeteria for George and no one was around so she gave him a big hug and kiss as the door closed behind him.

"Wow," George smiled.

"I'm going to have to help Mr. Crenshaw pack up of few things, but before I do, I just wanted to tell you how proud I am of you and the job you have done here. It's no wonder I fell for you. I can't wait for my folks to meet you. But now, I'd better get down there and help get ready to evacuate. Stop by and see Mr. Crenshaw if you have time. He really likes you. Bye for now, honey," Laura said. She was so excited and it showed when she talked so fast. It almost made George laugh.

George went to the chopper to wait for Lt. Dewitt and the volunteers, and when he arrived, he asked him, "Would you please have four of your men act as guards for those who are setting the charges and the loading onto the chopper. Make sure that they know that they must join us when we board the chopper. Make sure they are all present and accounted for."

Lt. Dewitt answered, "Of course, sir."

"A question, do you feel that what we did was a success, despite our losing Farrago?

Dewitt thought for a second and then replied, "Yes, sir, I believe it was a total success, but I should never have lost my man."

"I must remind you once again that I took care of that with HQ," George reminded him. "No one knows about it but you and Harry and me. We will not to speak of it ever outside this compound. And after we leave this matter here, Lieutenant," George said as he looked intently at him, "I think you are a great officer. You are an honorable man. If I had a daughter, from what I know about you, I would want her to have a husband with such a character as yours."

"Why, thank you, sir," Dewitt said, smiling, "I will take that as a great compliment. And believe me, sir, right now, I really, really need a vote of confidence."

Just then, Sgt. Decker entered the office. "Well done, sirs. You two have done a great job, and it has been a privilege to work with you both." He saluted them both. They responded in like manner.

George spoke first, "Thank you for your kind words, Sergeant. I would like to commend you on your skills on clarifying those pictures, both of the Davenport and Farrago."

"Thanks, Captain," Decker said, shaking his head. "You know I've been thinking about his escape. It's strange about the timing of his escape, how it occurred just as things worked out with the fireworks, wasn't it?"

"It sure was, Sgt. Decker," George responded while shaking his head, "I was just explaining to Lt. Dewitt how that that subject should not ever be spoken of again. Don't you think that is best for him?"

"Yes, sir," Decker said, "and I concur with that advice, but it almost seemed that it was an inside job."

"Why don't you explain that to the lieutenant?" George said as he stood to leave. "It just might take some pressure off Lt. Dewitt, and I don't want that to continue to bother him. The responsibility really lies on my shoulder anyway. As you know, the buck stops here. So cheer him up before we set the charges in the facility this evening, but remember, it's over after that, Sgt Decker. I'll meet you in a few minutes at the runway."

George stood and shook hands with both men. "I hope to work with both of you again one day. God bless you both."

# The Final Moments

## Day 18

In the staging area near the runway, Sgt. Grant stopped George.

"Captain, your men believe that you are a great leader and your heart is with your men. We all noted that you are a religious man, so we want to give you and your beautiful wife an autographed Holy Bible. I say autographed because every man and woman in your company has signed it. Every member of the civilian work force has added their signatures. You thanked us, but now let us give you just a token of our appreciation for your leadership before we get on those choppers."

Then someone started. "Hip, hip, hurrah! Hip, hip, hurrah." Then they sang, "For he's a jolly good fellow, for he's a jolly good fellow. Which nobody can deny, which nobody can deny…"

Laura looked into his eyes as they continued to sing, then she whispered the words, "I love you and I agree with them."

George stood. "Thank you all for your vote of confidence and the Bible, Laura and I will always cherish it. I will meet you in a short while on the ship that is waiting for us."

Lt. Dewitt burst through the door and announced that the first group of fourteen civilians was to prepare to board the waiting Black Hawk. Laura and George grabbed their things and headed for the waiting helicopter. George waved good-bye as Laura boarded the first chopper under the sound of whirring blades. Captain Lee walked to where Sgt Collins waited with his men.

"Sergeant, please get these explosives off that helicopter."

The blades slowed as Collins and his men hurriedly but carefully loaded the explosives on to a waiting cart. As soon as the cart had cleared the landing area, the second group of civilians began boarding. After they had all boarded, the helicopter lifted off. As it did, the next aircraft landed. This routine was to continue until all the civilians and military personnel were removed except the men still busy setting the charges.

Inside the building, soldiers were busily setting the charges as they had been instructed. When a soldier had completed setting his assigned charges, he headed for the terminal to await the other men before boarding the last copter. By the time the last helicopter was heard, all but one soldier had completed their job. Sgt. Collins went to check on his progress. He entered a hallway yelling, "Corporal Higgins, are you all right?"

He heard a moan. He opened a door and there lay Higgins with a pack of C-4 clutched tightly in his left hand. "What happened?" Collins asked.

Higgins answered weakly, "I tripped over a broom or something and fell and banged my head against the corner of the dresser."

Collins said, "Hand me the C-4!" He grabbed it and laid it softly on the bed and reached out to help Higgins. "Sorry, Sergeant, but I can't seem to move."

"All right, Higgins, just stay here and relax. I will place the charges and then help you get out of here." Harry quickly placed the remaining two charges in the next two rooms, then returned and lifted Corporal Higgins on his back. He carried him over his shoulders until they reached the men waiting for them. Two men ran to assist Sgt. Collins. Fortunately, there was a medic aboard the chopper. After they loaded Higgins aboard and everyone was aboard, they lifted off. As they leveled off, the medic checked his Higgins's pulse.

143

"Captain, I think I'd better start an intravenous drip. As soon as we land, we need to get this man medical attention."

"All right, corpsman, see to it that he gets what he needs," George ordered as he pulled the activating device from its pouch. He looked over at the pilot and asked the distance from the facility. After the pilot told him that they should be far enough away, George yelled, "Fire in the hole."

In about a minute, the night sky lit up as bright as day.

"Thank God we are out of there. None of us would have survived such devastation. Elated cheers resounded as they headed into the night. Relieved that they had finished the assignment, he now looked forward to taking Laura in his arms.

# THE AFTERMATH

After the copter landed on an aircraft carrier, George and his men headed to meet with the earlier arrivals. They were waiting near the aircraft elevators. As he walked toward them, the captain of the carrier exited a nearby door and waited to greet him. As he neared the captain, the ship's captain called, "Attention."

At his command, all branches of service snapped to attention. "Welcome aboard, Captain Lee. I am Captain James Manning, captain of the aircraft carrier, USS *Idaho*, and this is my executive officer, Commander Charles Thombler. Sir, it is an honor to have you aboard." He turned to the group and ordered, "At ease." As everyone relaxed, he continued, "We are awaiting the arrival of another ship which can better accommodate all your people and get you to some military facility on the mainland. Colonel Murphy told me to give you his regards and tell you that he will see you soon."

"Thank you for your greeting, sir," George began, "but I feel that it is I who should be saluting you."

"Nonsense, Captain, after what I've heard about you, you and your teams and how you possibly may have prevented a war, I don't think so. No telling how many lives you will have saved. The satellite launch is scheduled in a few hours. That's when you will see the results of your work in action."

Out of the corner of his eye, George caught a glimpse of Laura heading his way. "Excuse me, but I have a VIP to greet, Captain."

Captain Manning turned toward the direction George was looking as Laura practically ran toward them.

"Oh, honey, how did it go? Did it go as planned? I'm so glad you made it."

"Hello, sweetheart, it went well."

George smiled as he turned toward the ship's captain. "I'd like you to meet Captain James Manning and his executive officer, Commander Thombler. Gentlemen, this is my wife, Laura Lee."

They both greeted Laura. "Well, Captain Lee, I guess you have dual roles to play now."

"Yes, sir," George grinned, "but I'm not sure I'm trained well enough in the recently acquired duty as husband. I am still in basic training and have a lot to learn, Captain Manning."

"Believe me, Captain Lee," the ship's captain commented as he looked at Laura and George, "I understand. Both Commander Thombler and I are married, and we struggle with that responsibility occasionally because it's mostly OJT. I will leave you two so you can catch up. It has been a pleasure to meet you both, and I wish you two the best in your marriage."

Soon, the USS *J. P. Jones* loomed into sight. There was quite a stir among Captain Lee's group as they caught sight of the 68,000-ton Harpers Ferry-class dock landing ship. George learned that there were 22 officers and almost 400 enlisted personnel on the ship. He had also learned that the Marine detachment had gone ashore so the ship could accommodate George's group. This made the ship's quarters available to them. After the transfer between ships, the captain of the USS *J. P. Jones* gave the order to turn about and head for the port in Los Angeles, California, at full speed. George knew that at 20 knots that it would take approximately 2 days to get to port. It was past time for breakfast by the time they got underway. Captain Samuel Dominique went to George's quarters and knocked on his door. Laura answered the door to his surprise.

"Why hello, ma'am, I am Captain Dominique, I was expecting Captain Lee to answer. I am sorry. I must have the wrong quarters."

"Oh no, sir," Laura quickly explained, "you have the right quarters. I am Mrs. Laura Lee. Captain Lee and I were recently married. Come in, sir."

George came out of the head and entered the room. "Yes, Captain Dominique, please do come in and have a seat. We are so fortunate that your ship came out to pick us up. Thanks for the accommodations."

"I just wanted to stop in and make an official welcome to our ship," Captain Dominique explained. "I've heard that you are quite a celebrity back in Washington, DC. I don't know what you and your people have done, but I've heard you may just have delayed a third world war. Anyway, you and your people are welcome aboard."

Captain Lee answered, "Thanks for the welcome, but maybe they have me mixed up with someone else, sir."

"That may be, Captain Lee," Dominique said, smiling, "but somehow, I doubt it. I also understand that you are not permitted to discuss anything about your assignment. Please, will you and your lovely wife join me at the captain's table for meals during our journey back to port?"

"We would be happy to do that, Captain Dominique. Thank you, sir," George replied.

"Good, then I will meet you in the mess deck in a few minutes," Dominique said. "Please excuse me."

When Laura and he had entered the mess deck, Captain Lee was surprised to find Sgt. Carter working with the crew's mess deck team.

"Good morning, Captain, has everyone been assigned quarters?"

"Yes, I think everyone is in quarters. Sgt. Carter, you certainly do work fast," George commented. "How did you get them to let you help?"

"Well, sir, they were short handed, so when I volunteered, they took me in like a wayward orphan. Hey, do you remember that quartet we formed earlier? If we could get something together, would it be okay if we gave a little concert this evening?"

"It sounds good to me, but we will have to get with the ship's captain for permission and a location for it to take place," George answered.

"If we are permitted, we will try to be prepared by 1700 hours this evening," Sgt. Carter advised.

"All right, we are dining with the captain so I will ask him," George said.

About that time, an ensign approached Laura and George.

"Sir, are you Captain Lee?"

George nodded. Then the ensign continued, "Would you and Mrs. Lee please follow me to the captain's table. They followed him over to the table and he pulled out a chair for Laura to be seated, and then the captain's chair, then he told them, "The captain sends his regrets that he will be delayed in joining you. He invites you to proceed without him. What would you like to order, sir?"

George ordered, "Eggs, bacon, white toast, and coffee, if that is available, Ensign Jordan."

"Yes, sir, that is available. And you, ma'am, what would you like?" he asked Laura.

"I'd like some oatmeal, toast, and sugar-free jelly," Laura responded. "And please make the toast white bread, toasted lightly."

The ensign asked, "And what would you like to drink, Mrs. Lee?"

Laura said, "I'll have a glass of milk, please."

The ensign thanked them and then headed off. In about five minutes, he returned with a small pot of coffee for George and a glass of milk for Laura. He also sat two coffee mugs on the table. The captain had arrived and was seating himself, so the ensign asked what he would like for breakfast.

"The usual, Ensign Jordan, thank you," the captain said, "and thanks for the coffee."

"You're welcome, sir. And your breakfast is coming right up, sir," Ensign Jordan said, looking at Captain Dominique.

"Well, I do hope you two are enjoying your stay on the ship, Captain," Dominique said politely. "Your company and the civilian personnel have been very well behaved, They get along with the Navy- and Marine-enlisted personnel far better that the Marine detachments usually do. There is far too much competition there, you know."

Both Laura and George laughed at those remarks.

George replied, "Yes, I suppose so, at least according to the rumors I've heard."

About that time, the food arrived. Laura and George bowed their heads and quietly offered thanks to God for the food they received. When they finished, Captain Dominique said, "Amen. Let's dig in."

George, during the course of the meal, asked Captain Dominique, "Captain, one of my men asked if it would be all right for his quartet to sing for the ship's personnel as well as our own group this evening at 1700 hours. Do you think that will be possible, sir?"

"Captain Lee, I think that will be a terrific idea," Captain Dominique responded enthusiastically. "It may be a morale booster for the ship's personnel. I will arrange for everything and have the stage set up with lights and a magnificent sound system, which one of the crew members has built. According to the weather reports, it should be clear tonight, so tell them they can have it on deck."

At the end of the meal, George was happy to give Sgt. Grant the good news. Sgt. Grant smiled from ear to ear.

"Please tell Laura that her friend and she should meet me here about an hour after breakfast to go over some songs, sir."

Laura and George left the mess deck for their quarters. They relaxed for a while and then someone knocked on the door. It was Laura's friend, Jesse Braden. They hugged.

"Are you ready to go practice?"

Laura nodded, stood, and gave George a hug and kiss, then left with Jesse. In a short while, there was another knock at the door. George opened it, and Ensign Jordan announced to George, "Sir, there is a phone call for you, please follow me."

George grabbed his jacket and cap. When he entered the room where the phone was waiting, he simply picked it up and said, "Captain Lee here."

On the other end, a familiar voice spoke, "Captain Lee, is the room clear?"

George informed Colonel Murphy that it was not. Then he asked Ensign Jordan, "Ensign, please have this room cleared so that I may talk in private to my CO."

It took a minute or so for everyone to clear the room. "Colonel Murphy, good morning, sir. What can I do for you, sir?"

"Good morning, Captain Lee. Primarily I just wanted to give you an update. At 0600 tomorrow, the unit you worked on will be headed skyward. We expect to have it operational within three hours of obtaining orbit. You can expect to hear the news by 1200 hours tomorrow, Captain. Inform the scientists and engineers about this. By the way, how is the young man with the head injury doing?"

"Sir," George replied, "Corporal Higgins is doing well. In fact, I saw him during breakfast. He had a big bandage on his head, but was laughing and cutting up with his buddies. Sir, I have a question for you. Are my parents and sister okay?"

"Captain, they are fine," Murphy replied. "And we have men posted around the buildings to make sure that no intruders get at them. To change the subject, after you arrive in Los Angeles, you and Laura will be escorted to Washington to receive the Medal of Honor as a reward for the successful completion of this mission. I will be there to present it myself. It will be great to see you again, Captain. Please give Laura my regards."

Captain Lee hung up and motioned Ensign Jordan to allow people back into the room. He thanked the ensign for his assistance and apologized for disturbing the men. The ensign saluted, George returned it, and then shook his hand. Then George headed back to his quarters.

Just before lunch, Laura returned looking happy. Shortly afterward, they headed for the mess deck for lunch. The lunch was uneventful, and the conversation with Captain Dominique was pleasant.

After they left the captain's table, George spotted Mr. Crenshaw and went over to him. He spotted Dr. Piton sitting at another table. There was an empty table between them so he invited them both to sit with him there. Just as the two men were seated, Sgt. Collins came up to greet Captain Lee.

"Hey, Sgt. Collins, you're just in time. Come join us for a minute. Have you seen Lt. Dewitt?"

"Yes, sir! I think he is sitting right over there."

Lt. Dewitt saw them looking in his direction and waved. Captain Lee motioned for him to join them. After they were all gathered at the table, George gave them the good news from Col. Murphy.

As they were leaving the table, the intercom came to life.

"Ladies and gentlemen, this is your captain speaking. Tonight at 1700 hours, there will be special entertainment on the main deck. Everyone is invited to come and enjoy an hour or so of entertainment with singing by a mixed Southern gospel quartet."

During the day, they repeated the announcement every two hours until after dinner at 1400 hours.

Laura and the captain went to their quarters until Laura needed to leave for a final practice. She returned about an hour before supper. She looked concerned.

"We practiced so long that I am afraid my voice will fail this evening."

"Ask Sgt. Carter for a slice of lemon to suck on after supper," George advised. "That just might help."

"Thanks, George, I forgot that old trick," Laura said as she brightened up. She reached up and pulled down George's head and gave him a lingering kiss. When they came up for air, she said, "George, the time I have spent with you have been the happiest times in my life. I didn't quite understand what this job was all about when I took it, but I'm so glad I did. This side benefit in and of itself has made it a worthwhile endeavor."

"I know what you mean." George smiled. "We would probably have never met if either one of us had failed to get this assignment. I usually don't make this kind of statement, but I feel that God may have ordained that we meet through this project. You have made me so happy that I do not feel worthy of such joy."

Once again, Laura reached up and kissed him. "I love you, you handsome man."

"I love you too, you beautiful lady," George told her as he drew her near once again. "Life is good."

Laura nursed a slice of lemon off and on during supper at the captain's table. The captain was cordial as usual.

"I'm looking forward to the Sing-fest this evening. It's been quite a while since someone has given us such an opportunity.

Laura responded as she swallowed the remnant of lemon juice, "We certainly hope you enjoy it. This will be our first public performance. We just recently formed the group."

Captain Dominique looked surprised. "Do you mean that you are a part of the singing group?

"I apologize that I had not informed you, but yes, sir, I am part of the quartet. I thought you probably already knew," she answered sincerely.

"No problem, ma'am," Captain Dominique stated. "Again, I can't wait to hear your first public performance. Make us proud. Now, if you will excuse me, duty calls."

The Lees chatted as they finished their meal. "Well, it won't be long now until the debut of your new career. Just think of it, from an engineer to a singing great with just a few practices. I can read the headlines now, 'Former engineer now staring in a remake of the Sound of Helicopters.' Maybe it should be called the 'Building Crew.'"

Laura playfully said, "I'll get you for this, you would-be comedian."

The quartet agreed to meet about twenty-five minutes before the concert. Laura paced nervously. "George, please pray for us, especially me, I'm as shaky as a leaf in a tornado."

George bowed his head and prayed for the group right then. By the time he had finished, the rest of the quartet had gathered round and were bowing their heads in prayer. They all thanked George. Laura brought one of her friends over.

"George, this is Cathy. She will be playing the piano for us. She once played with one of the big name symphony orchestras."

"I'm glad to meet you, Cathy, I suppose you know already that my name is George," George said, smiling.

Cathy smiled. "Yes, sir, I have heard a lot about you since before the 'big day.' Mind you, it was nothing bad. It was all good, but I had an inside source."

"I'm sure you did," George said as he looked over at Laura with a half grin.

Laura immediately interjected herself in the situation, "Cathy, don't you think it's about time to leave?

They all laughed as Cathy agreed, "Yes, I suppose so. He is cute, just like you said."

Laura grabbed her by the arm and with a smile she gave George a quick kiss and she pushed Cathy toward the door.

At 1700 hours, Captain Dominique welcomed everyone and wished them a good time. He then turned the show over to the quartet. They sang a song, then they had an invocation. After that, they sang four hymns and a few contemporary songs. They felt that they should take a ten-minute break. As they walked off the stage, a band made up of three sailors played. When the quartet returned to the stage, there were cheers and lots of clapping. Sergeant Carter stood and waved for them to stop.

"Ladies and gentlemen, we have a surprise for you. Where is Captain Lee? Captain Lee, please come up on the stage."

Cheers resounded across the waves as Captain Lee reluctantly climbed the steps to the stage. Sgt. Carter motioned for him to come over to where he stood. A member of the group handed Sgt. Carter another mike. He handed it to George.

"I may pay for this later, but we just had to do this. As most of you may know, Captain Lee is a terrific officer, but something you may not know is that Captain Lee has a wonderful voice. It must be that boyhood country air with all the goats, chicken, pigs, horses, and cows that he had to call into the barn to feed that gave him a good start." The audience roared with laughter. "Captain Lee, would you lead all of us in that old hymn, 'Amazing Grace?'"

George took the microphone and said, looking at Sgt. Carter, "You're right about one thing, Sergeant, you definitely will pay for this."

Laughter spread over the audience again. Then George smiled. "Just kidding. Have you heard the one about the pigeon and the dove?"

Boos rose from the soldiers.

"Okay, I won't try that. All right, let's stand and sing together one of my favorite old hymns. He looked over at Cathy. "Cathy, if you would give an introduction." She played the introduction beautifully, then George began, "Amazing grace, how sweet the sound, that saved a wretch like me."

As he continued to lead the hymn, tears filled the eyes of many of those standing in the audience. Laura beamed with pride as she sang along. She thought, *I am the luckiest woman in the world.*

These were the thoughts of a woman who was deeply in love.

The words, "When we've been there ten thousand years, we've no less days to sing God's praise," were among

George's favorite words. Tears filled his eyes as he recalled as a teenager, how he had gone forward at the little Wesleyan Church and surrendered to God's will and allowed His amazing grace to enter his own heart. When the singing stopped, the crowd clapped wildly. George turned to walk off the stage.

Sgt. Carter caught up to George and said, "Just a minute, sir, there's something else. The quartet wants you to sing one song with us." Then he turned to the audience, "What do you folk say?"

Cheers began and kept going as they chanted, "Captain Lee, Captain Lee," over and over until he turned back and agreed. The quartet was already in place when George joined them.

Laura looked at George, smiled, and whispered, "Honey, I told you I'd get you."

George smiled, and whispered, "You really have."

The pianist introduced "The Star Spangled Banner." Soldiers and sailors and the few Marines that were aboard stood at attention and saluted and civilians stood and held their right hands over their hearts and the US flag was marched to the center of the stage by the honor guards and the quintet began, "Oh say, can you see, by the dawn's early light..."

After the anthem, the military held their salutes until the flag was marched off the stage and out of sight. Someone ordered, "At ease, as you were." Everyone clapped again as George left the platform.

Sgt. Carter said, "Thank you, Captain Lee, for doing that." Then he turned to the crowd and addressed them, "Just because he has a great voice and knows Christian hymns does not mean that you will get away with crossing swords with him. He is combat seasoned. I've seen him in action, so it is best if you show him the respect he deserves."

Everyone was still clapping as the quartet continued the concert.

After the concert, George and Laura were having a cup of Java in their quarters as they reviewed the evening's events.

George commented, "Cathy sure is a gifted musician. And the quartet did a tremendous job tonight. The crowd loved it."

"I know, honey, and you just blew them away," Laura bragged. "You have a beautiful voice, my love."

"Your voice is great," George commented. "I suppose we should try a duet some time."

Laura, in her usually bubbly manner, suggested, "How about right now?"

George named a song and Laura nodded, then began singing.

George joined in and then stopped. "I think I should lead." Then they started over again.

They felt that they sang beautifully together and they did so until it was past time to retire for the evening.

# Day 19

*The alarm went off way to early*, George thought as he reached for the snooze bar.

Laura reached over and gave George a hug. "Good morning, love. It's time to get back to the old grind."

"After last night, I do not want to face our people," George said. "I am just too embarrassed."

"Oh, sugar, you were super last night," Laura said hopefully. "We'll go have some breakfast, and you will see how well they liked it."

As they entered the cafeteria, George and Laura saw that Sergeant Carter was among the serving crew. He waved as they came through they door.

"Hello, Captain and Mrs. Lee. I think you're going to enjoy the waffles this morning because I kind of the made the mix from one of my own special recipes. And, Captain, I just wanted you to know that I really enjoyed your singing last night. You're the talk of the ship. And, Laura, you are an asset to the quartet."

"Thanks, Allen," Laura said. "I can see why you were in a professional quartet, you can reach way down into the basement. Last night was so much fun that Captain Lee and I sang duets until we went to bed."

"Well, what about that? I imagine it was good," Allen responded. "You guys will have to sing for us sometime, Laura."

George smiled but shook his head. "I don't think so. Public singing makes me nervous. I think I get less nervous preparing for a battle."

They left Sgt. Carter to his serving and headed over to the captain's table. As they were seated, Ensign Jordan hurried up to the table.

"What would you like this morning, Captain and Mrs. Lee?" Before they could answer, Ensign Jordan commented, "You two did a great job last night. You did your group from the aircraft carrier proud, sir. Now, what would you like?

"Sgt. Carter said something about waffles being available, perhaps that would be good, with a couple eggs and bacon," Captain Lee ordered.

"They are delicious," Ensign Jordan said. "I had four, they were so good. Would you like some, Mrs. Lee?"

Laura nodded, and Ensign Jordan turned to get their drinks. The ensign returned in about three minutes. "The coffee smells great. Captain Dominique will probably love it."

Laura agreed and began sipping on hers. "Not only does the coffee smell good, it tastes good too."

About that time, Captain Dominique arrived and sat down at the table and greeted everyone. As usual he was in an enjoyable mood. "Good morning, everyone, how are you folk today?"

Laura answered, "I'm well, and you, sir?"

Captain Dominique replied, "I'm terrific. How about our baritone singer, George, is it okay with you?"

"Yes, I suppose so. I kind of didn't want to face the world after last night, though."

"George, if I had a voice like yours, I'd retire and go into singing full-time," Dominique said. "Isn't that right, Ensign Jordan?"

Jordan replied, "If I were blessed with his talent, I wouldn't have joined Navy, sir."

"Come on, gentlemen, you can stop teasing me now," George said, bowing his head.

"No, sir! I'm not kidding, it was great last night," Jordan said sincerely.

About that time, Sgt. Carter arrived with a tray while two others held a couple more.

"Lady and gentlemen, here are some of the most delicious pancakes this side of the Mason/Dixon line."

George and Laura bowed their heads and offered thanks to God for their food. After they finished, they all dug in.

Almost in union, the all said, "Sgt. Carter, these really are delicious."

"We told you so, didn't we?" Ensign Jordan said. "Now you can see why I had four."

Breakfast continued with very little conversation because everyone was savoring the delicious waffles. When they finished, Captain Dominique told George, "You know, Captain Lee, I think we ought to have Sgt. Carter transferred from the Army to the Navy. What do you think?" They all had a good laugh.

Sgt. Carter shook his head. "I couldn't do that. Captain Lee here needs me to keep him energized so that he can keep running to all those promotion celebrations."

Breakfast ended when Captain Dominique rose from the table and excused himself.

Just before lunch, Ensign Jordan came and asked Captain Lee to follow him to the phone.

George answered, "Hello, Captain Lee here."

"Good morning, Captain Lee, this is Colonel Murphy, I just wanted to let you know that you will have a car waiting for you at the dock. There will also be car for Mr. James Crenshaw and Dr. Charles Piton, who will be taken to a local hotel for debriefing. Leave First Lieutenant Patrick Dewitt in charge of the troops. He will supervise the loading on to transports and convoy taking them to a nearby military base. You and Mrs. Lee will be escorted to the airport and taken to watch the launch of the object. I will meet you two there. Best of luck, Captain, and we will see you soon, Captain Lee. Good-bye for now."

Gorge told Laura at lunch about their surprise flight to the launch. Captain Dominique wished them well.

Captain Lee asked Ensign Jordan if he would locate Lt. Dewitt and bring him to his table. It didn't take long for Jordan to return with Dewitt. Dewitt greeted Captain Lee and was invited to sit. George told him that he was to take charge of the soldiers and prepare them for transport to the unannounced location.

"The civilians will be sent somewhere to await the trip back to locations near their homes."

Lt. Dewitt shook hands and expressed his gratitude for the opportunity to work with him. George wished him the best, then to the lieutenant's surprise, he stood and saluted him, and then shook his hand again as he told him good-bye.

The rest of the day passed quickly, and sure enough, there were cars awaiting Dr. Piton and Mr. Crenshaw. There were three military buses waiting for the civilians. The ten six-by trucks soon filled with soldiers who were headed for chow to be served at some still unknown location. Captain Dominique walked Laura and George to the walkway off the ship.

"Thanks for the lift, Captain Dominique, it has been a pleasant journey. You are a gracious host. That Ensign Jordan you had helping Laura and me is a good man, sir. He will make a good career Navy man with your guidance."

"I agree, Captain Lee. Before you go, let me tell you that it has been an honor to meet you and Laura Lee. Laura, I wish you many happy years with this man," Captain Dominique said, saluted, and turned and walked away.

A lieutenant greeted George and Laura at the bottom of the gangway. "Welcome ashore, Captain Lee, sir, and Mrs. Lee, ma'am. Please follow me."

He led them to a vehicle, opened the door for them, and they got into the back. The tickets were ready when they arrived at the airport and they were hurried through airport security which carried their luggage through without x-raying it at the ire of other boarders. Soon, the plane taxied toward the runway while Captain and Mrs. Lee were anticipating a meal in first class.

## Day 20

It was just past midnight when the plane landed. There had been a stop over in St. Louis before they arrived at Orlando, Florida. After they deplaned, they chatted with Colonel Murphy as two officers retrieved their luggage and loaded them into the trunk of a waiting vehicle. After they all got inside, the driver headed for their motel.

After forty-five minutes, they arrived at their motel and in Cocoa Beach where they already had rooms registered in their names. They were happy to get a few hours' rest before they headed for the Cape Canaveral Air Force Station's launch site. The next morning, an officer awakened them to inform them it was time for breakfast. They enjoyed a delicious breakfast with Colonel Murphy and his aide. When they finished eating, they headed for the Cape. They parked near Space Launch Complex 37, located a safe distance from the launch pad.

Colonel Murphy explained, "The satellite sits atop a Galaxy One Saturn Rocket and as we speak, we are approaching the final countdown before launch. After it obtains orbit, it should be ready to destroy of the enemy's weapon. We have discovered its location but a standard missile would be unable to reach the deeply implanted device. With the newly devised weapon and its unique sighting mechanism that your team mounted on the satellite, we should be able to destroy it the moment it comes into satellite view."

George and Laura listened intently as the colonel continued to describe the launch routine.

"I'm sure you understand the importance of this launch. This may make the difference between halting a war," Murphy explained. "And if all goes well, you and your crews will be credited to its prevention. Either way, Captain, I'm proud of everyone efforts." He thought a moment, "I'll let you two in on a little secret. Tomorrow, we will fly to Washington, DC, and you will be presented the Medal of Honor by President Clyde Whinton himself. Later, we will dine with him and the First Lady at the White House."

"Are you serious? We are dining with President Whinton and the First Lady, "Laura said. "Wow, this is all happening way too fast. It's all making my head swim."

"Really, Colonel Murphy," George said, "I really do not deserve all this."

"My boy, I think you do and so does the president," Murphy said, "and you really don't want to cross swords with the president, do you?"

George replied, "No, sir, I don't suppose it would be appropriate to contradict the commander-in-chief."

Murphy advised, "Well, why don't you just try and relax and everything will turn out fine. Just go with the flow."

George and Laura read some of the brochures about the planned launches that were pending. They even had tickets available for purchase to take scheduled space flights. Murphy soon informed them that the missile launch countdown was nearing completion. About that time, Mr. Crenshaw and Dr. Piton arrived at the viewing platform and the trio stood to greet them.

"Welcome," Colonel Murphy said. "It is a pleasure to see you both again. Come join us."

Dr. Piton shook his head. "No, it is our pleasure, Colonel Murphy. And, Captain and Mrs. Lee, we didn't know what had become of you two."

Mr. Crenshaw also shook hands then added, "Imagine our surprise when we saw you two up here with Colonel Murphy. It's almost like a reunion. I can't wait until we see this thing going into orbit. I'm so excited. This is such an important launch that I'm a nervous wreck."

Dr. Piton and Mr. Crenshaw each gave Laura a hug. They tried to make small talk, but everyone felt the pressure building as the launch time neared. The fate of their world was weighing on their shoulders.

Finally, the countdown was down to ten seconds, "10…9…8…" continued until it reached "0, ignition."

Blazing fuel lifted the rocket with its secret payload off the launch pad, at first very slowly, and then its acceleration rapidly, constantly increasing speed until it disappeared into the morning sky.

As everyone clapped, Laura jumped to her feet. "Wow, that was awesome, the neatest thing I have ever seen."

Colonel Murphy replied, "Well, it's routine for those who work with this daily, but to us watching for the first time, it definitely is exciting. Now we have to wait for a report on its orbit. Come with me to the control room."

They entered a room where they could see the myriad of computers and personnel that it takes to achieve successful launches.

Laura whispered, "George, it's because of you that I am allowed to see how these things work." She looked around and quickly sneaked him a kiss on the cheek.

Things seemed tense in the control room, but the launch had been successful. The first rocket section separated, then the second, and then the satellite was on its own.

Finally, the launch supervisor announced, "The solar panels have deployed and stationary orbit has been achieved."

Cheers and clapping could be heard through the glass that separated the observers from the control room. Everyone was elated at the success of the launch. George wondered if anyone knew how truly important this launch was.

By the time Colonel Murphy, his aide, Laura, and George returned to the staff car, the Air Force had transferred control of the satellite to army controllers that were in a secret location. They were tasked with the destruction of the enemy's weapon when the opportunity presented itself. George later learned that Dr. Piton and Mr. Crenshaw had been taken to the army's fire control facility to assist with initiating the firing since they had prior experience and had taken part in the test firing on the island. As he heard that news, George felt a surge of pride for his colleagues. For now, there was nothing for them to do but go to their quarters at Patrick Air Force Base. Colonel Murphy sat in the back and chatted with George as they traveled the few miles to their motel. Laura could not believe how beautiful the ocean was as she looked out over the bay on one side and the Atlantic Ocean on the other.

George told them that his parents had come here on vacation when Charlene and he were small children and that there had been only a couple of small motels back then. An Air force test plane had crashed on the beach near their motel. He had heard the roar of the twin engines increase as the plane plunged downward toward the beach. They passed the crash site on the way to lunch and the black smoke was still rising from the crashed plane. At the time, his childish mind was amazed that all the brass had gathered and could not understand why there were so many. He concluded his reminiscing as they neared base guard post.

"Now, I understand the reason for all the security and brass back then."

The guard saluted as the staff car pulled to a stop at the entrance of the base. He quickly checked the vehicle and checked the list of names the OIC (officer in charge) had given him.

"Please state your names!" They each in turn called their rank and names and presented their IDs. Laura stated her name and showed her driver's license. George stated that she was his wife. The sergeant checked off their names as they were called out. Finally, he saluted and waved them ahead.

The quarters were similar to those they had stayed in on the island, so they felt right at home. George and Laura flopped down on the bed, gave each other a hug and kiss, and quickly fell asleep in each other's arms.

## Day 21

It seemed like only a few minutes until Colonel Murphy's aide's knocking awakened them.

"Captain and Mrs. Lee, it's time to have breakfast and head for Washington, sir."

Captain Lee opened the door and greeted the lieutenant, "Good morning Lieutenant, give us a few minutes, and we will meet you downstairs."

"Yes, sir, I will wait downstairs. Colonel Murphy will meet you at the mess hall, sir," the officer said. He saluted, turned, and left to wait on them.

It took a few minutes for them to freshen up and take care of personal hygiene. Hand in hand, they headed to the elevator. At the lobby, the elevator doors opened and George carried their larger bags until the lieutenant spied them. He rose immediately, rushed over, and offered to carry their bags for them.

George said, "I will take mine, and you can carry Laura's, Lieutenant."

It wasn't long until they were at the base.

As they entered the mess hall, they heard a familiar voice.

"Good morning," Colonel Murphy cheerfully greeted them. "Well, this is the big day, Captain Lee. We are scheduled for take-off in about a couple of hours. Are you excited?"

Laura and George returned the greeting and George answered, "I'm not sure. I really do not feel that I deserve such a great honor. After all, it was the people with the hands-on work that accomplished this."

"You are right about your crew, but they will be rewarded," Murphy said with a smile. "Every civilian who worked on the project will be given a nice bonus, and each member of the military will receive a promotion."

"Does that mean that First Sergeant Collins will become a second lieutenant?" George asked excitedly. "And First

Lieutenant Dewitt will be made a captain? That's great!" Then he turned to Laura, "Congratulations, honey, maybe you can buy that new car we talked about?"

Laura smiled. "That would be great, but right now, I'm famished, so let's eat."

One of the cooks brought their meals on a tray and was placing them on the table.

After the meal, they headed for the airfield where they boarded a small jet that seated ten or so people. There was only one passenger, a general, besides the five with Murphy's group. After they arrived at Atlanta, the general got off before them and headed for the terminal. The five of them boarded another flight for Washington, DC. Soon, they started the approach into Reagan National Airport, in Arlington, Virginia, across the Potomac from the nation's capital. From there, a staff car took them over to the White House, where President and Mrs. Whinton greeted them at the entrance. The president was a pleasant man, slightly balding, and walked with a hint of a limp. His wife had a winsome personality and a bright smile. The First Couple led them to the dining room where they were seated as the staff pulled their chairs out for each of them and waited for them to be seated. Laura glanced at George with a "wow" look. They had never been treated so royally before.

After they were seated, President Winton looked over at George and said, "I understand that you are a Christian and that you and your wife offer thanks before you eat. Would you do the honors and offer thanks for our food?"

George agreed and bowed his head. "Oh, God, please bless this food to the nourishment of our bodies. And, Lord, give President and Mrs. Whinton help as they guide our great nation. And please, God, would you give the president wisdom and guidance in the daunting days that lie ahead. Please give my associates who helped with the creation of this new mechanism and the assistance needed as they attempt to utilize the recently launched equipment. We ask this in the only name by which we can receive salvation, in the name of your Son, Jesus the Christ. Amen."

Most all those gathered at the table responded, "Amen."

Mrs. Whinton said, "My name is Colleen. It was so good to hear a sincere prayer. Thank you Captain Lee." Turning to Laura, she continued, "You are a very lucky woman to have found a true Christian for a husband."

"I know! He is one in a million, Mrs. Whinton. God has really blessed me with a man of such good character. But as you probably already know, he is definitely not perfect. I still have a bit of work to do to make that happen."

The two ladies had a good laugh.

President Whinton laughingly said, "My wife has been trying that on me for forty-five years, and it still hasn't happened." Again, there were some chuckles. "Christians are not perfect, but as you all know, our nation was founded on biblical principles. In fact, initially most or our laws intentionally or not were based on the Ten Commandments. It's too bad that some within our own ranks are some who are trying to rid our nation of anything to do with God, Christ, or Christianity. A man or woman who is a Christian simply cannot leave his Christ or Christian principles and morals outside while working. That includes an office in the White House, Congress, or the Senate during these days. We have tried to push God out of our country. It's no wonder we are in such dire straits and may be close to another war. What can we expect when we, as it were, spit in the face of God Himself."

"Mr. President, it is so good to hear a man of your position say words that are so encouraging," George said. "And by God's grace, if you can gain enough support, you just may be able to turn our nation back from the brink of destruction. Laura and I will pray to that end."

Mrs. Whinton said, "This topic is kind of scary, so let's change the topic as we eat, what about that?" They all agreed and almost simultaneously reached for their forks.

"My, this certainly is delicious," Laura said. "Your kitchen staff is quite skilled in cuisines."

"I know. If I lose my job, I guess I will have to send Mrs. Whinton to chef's school," President Whinton said. "But sometimes, I miss plain old country food like cornbread and beans. Being from near the Mason-Dixon Line, I was raised on that kind of fixins."

"Why, honey," Mrs. Whinton said, "they would fix us those things if you asked them too."

"I know, darlin', but I thought you liked this kind of stuff," he replied. "Okay," he continued with a wave of his hand, "Captain Lee, I guess you know why you are here. When that weapon destroys the enemy's super weapon, you will probably have prevented the beginning of the apocalypse. It will be an honor and privilege to place a medal of honor on you this afternoon, my boy."

"I appreciate the honor you are bestowing on me, but it was a unified effort of everyone in our group, Mr. President," George protested.

"I understand, but as you know, you were the man in charge on site," the president replied, "and if it had failed, I guess we would have faulted Colonel Murphy." They all laughed. "What do you have to say, Colonel Murphy?"

"Mr. President, it is one of the highest privileges in my life to be seated at your table," Colonel Murphy replied, "but this young couple was far more instrumental in the success of this mission than I. They were the key to getting the job done."

"Your people did a great job in selecting such skilled people to make this thing work, Colonel," President Whinton said with a look of admiration. "We'll all have desert in a bit, but now, Captain and Mrs. Lee, we have a surprise for you." The doors swung open and in paraded both sets of parents and Charlene. Tears welled up in

Laura's eyes as she jumped to her feet, let out a quiet scream, and ran over to hug her parents. George stood and walked over to his family and gave each one a hug. Mrs. Murphy entered, and Colonel Murphy's false teeth almost fell out.

President Whinton motioned, and staff came from several directions and guided the families to their seats. Piping hot food was brought and placed before them as he said a few words, "My wife and I welcome the parents of this fine couple and Colonel Murphy's wife into our dining room.

"After you finished eating, we will assemble in another room which is of adequate size and give these men further honors. So enjoy the rest of your meal while my wife and I excuse ourselves to prepare for the ceremony."

Everyone stood as President and Mrs. Whinton left. Things seemed a bit more relaxed with the president and his wife gone. Laura moved over and sat by her mother while George excused himself from the seat next to colonel and Mrs. Murphy and went over and sat between his parents. They continued to visit until a major entered the room and announced that the president was now awaiting his guest's arrival.

"Please follow me, ladies and gentlemen."

When they entered the room where the president and his wife were waiting, the families were shown to their seats while Colonel Murphy and George were escorted to a seat near the president's chair. None of the guests had ever seen so many military officers in one place. The chiefs of all the branches of the military were there from the Pentagon and were in full dress uniforms with all their ribbons and medals.

The president stood, and of course, the whole room rose to their feet.

"Ladies and gentlemen, we are gathered here to present medals and awards for outstanding service to our country. These, along with their people, accomplished the impossible and with God's help, that accomplishment may avert a holocaust. Colonel John Murphy, please step forward."

Colonel Murphy looked flabbergasted because he had not expected to receive a medal. He gathered his composure and stood, stepped out, made a right-face, and marched up before the president, did another right-face, stopped, and saluted the commander-in-chief. President Whinton returned the salute, turned, picked up the medal, and pinned it on the colonel's jacket.

"Colonel John Murphy, it is my privilege to give you this Medal of Honor as a token of our gratitude for your leadership in expediting the building of a defensive weapon capable of destroying a recently discovered new super weapon that is being prepared for use against our nation. Thank you for your outstanding service." Everyone stood and cheered and clapped. "Oh, I almost forgot. As a further token of our appreciation, you are being promoted to the rank of brigadier general."

The president shook hands with the colonel and gave him some papers. Murphy took one step back, saluted, did a right-face, and marched back to his seat beside George.

President Whinton turned from watching General Murphy. "And now, a man who worked in league with Colonel Murphy and successfully completed the mission to design and build a completely new device capable of destroying the enemy's weapon from orbit, Captain George Lee."

George proceeded in the same manner as the colonel had and stood before President Whinton.

The president began, "Ladies and gentlemen, we would have had more of a public ceremony, except this man has hopefully convinced our enemies that he and everyone with him has been killed by one of their spies. That's why this ceremony is so secret. Due to his leadership and planning, the mission was a success." He turned and picked up a medal. "Captain, no. Let me change that, Major George Lee, for your valiant efforts and leadership and ability to inspire your company of soldiers and civilians to complete a job that we had projected would take six months in less than a month. We present to you this Medal of Honor." He shook George's hand. "Congratulations, Major Lee. Wait! Before you go, I have something else." He turned toward Laura. "Mrs. Lee, please come join your husband."

Laura could not keep her mouth closed as she made her way to the president. As she approached him, the president turned and retrieved another medal. "For your suggestions to your superiors in the engineering section, ones that facilitated the rapid development of the device and facilitated less weight on the device, which saved thousands of dollars in sending it into orbit, I want you to have the Medal of Service, a medal which I have authorized just for this occasion."

Tears were running down her cheeks as the president pinned the medal on her blouse. She simply could not help herself. She turned and buried her head in George's chest. George could do nothing but hug her as the president announced, "Please join us for refreshments back in the dining room. Everyone is welcome."

Finally, George and Laura were able to return to the side of General and Mrs. Murphy.

"Congratulations, General Murphy," George said as he extended his hand and then hugged Mrs. Murphy.

Murphy shook George's hand and then Laura's. "Congratulations, Major and Mrs. Lee. George, it has really been an honor serving with you."

"Sir, you had some great ideas that were immensely important," George said. "And I feel it is an honor to have served under your command, sir."

The officers from the Pentagon shook hands with the honorees and wished them the best. The naval chief shook George's hand and smiled, "Major, if you ever get tired of being a grunt, give me a call and we will get you into a real career in the Navy. I heard from the ships you were aboard, and I want you to know that you are 'the man' in eyes of those captains."

"Thank you, sir. Captains Manning and Dominique and their staffs were very gracious and kind to me and my people," George said. "If all your ships are under such skilled captains, if we have a war, they will control the seas."

For an instant, George thought he noticed a familiar face. He racked his brain to recall who it might be. Finally, it dawned on him. "Farrago, that's who that was." He searched the whole room, but could not locate him.

After the festivities had gone on for a while, the president got everyone's attention. As they turned to listen, he began, "Ladies and gentlemen, I have just received some great news. I'm relieved to tell you that our intelligence has just verified the fact that our primary target has been destroyed. The device that our honorees and their teams of soldiers and civilians worked on so dutifully has accomplished its intended goal. If our work had been delayed even one more day, it may have been too late to prevent a war. The news of this huge success gives us even more reason for a celebration."

Everyone clapped with excitement over the news that most likely meant that WWIII had been averted.

The president continued, "Thank you all for coming and you may stay as long as you wish. My wife and I have a big day tomorrow, so we are going to excuse ourselves. We have to get our beauty sleep. This bit of good news makes a great conclusion to these festivities. Once again, congratulations to our three honored guests, and again, I thank you for coming. Good night, ladies and gentlemen."

President and Mrs. Whinton came over to the Lees and wished them many happy years together. Mrs. Whinton gave Laura a hug and whispered something in her ear. They both looked at each other and laughed aloud. George was curious, but did not pursue the matter. The president went over and shook hands with the Murphys.

Then the general came over and asked, "Are you two love birds ready to escape this party?"

"Yes, sir. Please allow us time to let our families know that we are heading back to the hotel," George requested.

Murphy agreed, and after the relatives were informed, they were about to leave. Murphy looked at the newlyweds. "Before we go, I want you to know that I think it's time that you two have a proper honeymoon. Don't you agree?"

George and Laura looked at each other, and George replied, "Yes, sir, Laura has been very patient, but I think that we should take time, if possible, to meet with the people who really made this happen. Also, I have another request, sir. Whatever duty assignment I am given, I would like to request that the newly promoted Lt. Collins be assigned with me. He is a good and loyal man, sir."

"Considering your past service together, I see no problem with granting your request, Major Lee," General

Murphy responded. "By the way, most civilians are still in California so you can meet with them when you meet with the soldiers that served under your command. Another thing, you have the privilege of informing them of the bonuses and promotions."

"That's wonderful, General Murphy," Major Lee said.

"I'll make the arrangement for Lt. Collins's assignment to your unit as soon as I get to my quarters," Murphy promised. "While we are at the Air Force base, it is an excellent time to pick up our new insignia. I will have my driver take you and Laura to the PX before he takes you to the family's hotel. I have to make some calls to get the ball rolling on your meeting with your people back in California. Perhaps that will get you nearer to a Hawaiian honeymoon. What about that? I'll make the arrangements and let you know when you should expect to leave."

When they arrived at their quarters, General Murphy's aide grabbed the general's bags and carried them inside. Murphy ordered the driver to take George to the PX before he took them to meet their families. George thanked Murphy, then he asked, "Do you want me to pick up some insignia for you while I'm there?"

He answered, "I'll have my aide do that, but thanks."

The trip to the PX didn't take long. George and Laura went in the main entrance. Laura was amazed and said, "I've never been inside one of these before. My! Look at all they have for sale. It's almost like shopping at the local mall, there is so much stuff."

George directed her toward the military insignia. He picked up twelve Major insignia and ten sew-on rank insignia for his fatigues. He did not purchase any branch insignia because he did not know which unit he would serve with.

He went to the checkout and paid for his purchases.

The cashier said, "Congratulations on your promotion, Major Lee, sir."

Major Lee said, "Thank you, young lady. You are pretty observant."

She replied, "My husband is an officer. He was assigned to some top secret mission. I haven't heard from him but once since he left. He couldn't tell me where he was headed or what he was doing, but it definitely was pretty important."

George asked, "What is your husband's name?"

"His name is First Lieutenant Patrick Dewitt," she answered proudly.

"What is an army bride doing working in an Air Force PX?" George acted surprised.

"Well, he was temporarily assigned as a liaison between his unit and the Air Force for directing air strikes in combat situations," the cashier said in a happy tone.

Laura had kept silent, but she felt she had to say something or simply burst, "I think we just might know your husband. We've been working with him."

George added, "And if it is the Lieutenant Patrick Dewitt we know, he was just promoted to the rank of captain. He hasn't been informed yet, but he will be when we meet with him. Another thing, he should be back with you in a few days because the mission has been successfully completed."

Hearing the news that her husband would be returning home, the cashier burst into tears, ran around to where George and Laura were stand, and gave them hugs all the while jumping up and down with excitement.

Laura asked, "What is your name, honey?"

She answered, "I'm so excited. My name is Kara Dewitt."

"If it is in fact your husband, we should see him in a day or so," George said with a smile.

"Before he left, he told me he would be acting as an MP platoon leader," Kara replied. "If you see him, please tell him I love him."

"Maybe you can tell him yourself in the near future, but if we do see him, we will be sure to give him your message, Kara," George advised Kara.

Kara asked, "I can see from your name tag that your last name is Lee, sir, but what is your first name?"

George looked surprised. "I'm sorry. I'm George and this is my wife of a couple weeks, Laura."

They shook hands and then Kara said, "I had better get back to work. It is so nice to meet you guys. I wish you a happy and long life together. I hope you are as happy as Patrick and I. Bye for now."

When the driver saw them coming out of the commissary, he hurriedly brought the vehicle over to pick them up. On the way to the parents' motel, George talked with the lieutenant and ascertained his name and where he was from: John Klink from Watertown, New York. He invited him to join them when they got there. He reluctantly accepted. They entered the restaurant where the families were waiting. They gave each other hugs and kisses. George introduced his sister Charlene to Lieutenant John Klink and they seemed to hit it off right away. George watched them out of the corner of his eye as they started talking. George smiled as he turned toward Mom and Dad.

"It is so good to see you away from all that military stuff, George," George's dad said. "Your boss, Laura, and you were the stars tonight. You know that when you told me you were on a top secret mission, I thought you were exaggerating a bit, but when you left in that whirlybird and those guys from the CIA came round, I was pretty well convinced that you were not."

Mom interrupted, "Now, Paul, I knew George wouldn't do that. From what President Whinton said tonight, what he did just might have saved us from another war. God love his heart, he must have worked so hard." She turned toward George and asked, "How many people did you have working for you, son?"

"Mom, I'm sorry, but I simply cannot tell you anything about that. What I can tell you is that I met my beautiful wife, Laura, during that time," Gorge answered.

"She sure is a lucky woman," George's mom stated firmly.

"I think I'm the lucky one, Mom," George said. "Just look at that woman. No other man is the world is as lucky as I, except maybe Dad."

They all had a chuckle as Mom reached over and gave George a kiss on the cheek. "You're so sweet, son."

"It's good you feel that way, son," Dad Lee said. "That's the way I still feel about your mom. Believe me, love softens a bad day. I haven't had to sleep with the sheep too often."

"Dad, I think you had better quit bragging on your relationship with Mom because I thought I saw a lamb reflected in Mom's eye just then," George warned.

Mom nodded as she reached past George and jabbed Paul in the ribs.

Laura enjoyed catching up on news from home while her mother beamed over the president's accolades.

"I am so proud of you, honey. I could never imagine ever having a chance to shake hands with President and Mrs. Whinton."

Her father said, "And we are glad that you found someone to spend the rest of her life with, but we are disappointed that you did not have a big wedding like we had always planned."

Laura explained, "It was almost love at first sight. He chased me until I caught him. When you get to know him, you will see that he is quite intelligent and a very honorable man. If necessary, he would give his life for me. The longer I know him, the more I love him."

The families continued visiting until George stood and hurried to the entrance where Dr. Piton and Mr. Crenshaw were entering. When Laura saw what was happening, she got up ran over to join George who was about to greet them. They welcomed them then asked, "What happened? We are glad to see you, but we thought you would be tied up with the Army for quite some time."

Dr Piton answered them, "Well, we did what was needed, and those Army people, who caught on very quickly, took over. We heard that Colonel Murphy and you two received medals from President Whinton. That must have been special for you all. Congratulations."

"Oh yes, it was such an honor to meet the President and First Lady. They are such a lovely couple," Laura answered.

George said, "Our parents are here, so why don't you come over and meet them."

They walked over to where the parents were sitting and Mr. Lee stood as George introduced them, "This is my dad and mom, Paul and Sally Lee. Mom and Dad, this is Dr. Charles Piton, one of the scientists that I had the privilege of working with, and this is Mr. James Crenshaw an associate of Laura's. These two men probably deserved the medal I received far more than I did."

By that time, Laura's parents had joined the group and heard the names of the men. George introduced Laura's parents to them and said, "I think that you may know Dr. Piton."

"Why, yes, we do," Simon Krieger said. "It's so good to see you again, Doctor. I'll have to talk to you a bit more about Major Lee and see if he has some deep dark secrets we may need to know about." He smiled and looked at George.

Mr. Crenshaw remarked, "I don't think Captain Lee stood a chance. I could tell that both of them were smitten when they first met, Simon. They were the talk of the town, so to speak. Everyone was so happy for them. I will however admit that it was a bit surprising when they got hitched so quickly."

"I guess some people know what they want when they see it," Dr. Piton said with a broad smile.

They all continued talking and drinking iced tea until someone mentioned the time. They agreed that it was time to get some rest. George realized that he had not introduced Charlene to Dr. Piton and Mr. Crenshaw, so when he finally found them, he asked Lt. Klink and Charlene to come over and meet them.

As they approached, George began, "Dr. Piton and Mr. Crenshaw, this is my sister Charlene Lee and Lieutenant John Klink, General Murphy's aide."

They both told Charlene that it was a pleasure to meet her and Lt. Klink. They excused themselves and headed next door to the hotel. George and Laura followed suit and told everyone good night. Lt. Klink stayed with Charlene until he saw George head for the door. He quickly gave Charlene a hug and told her that he would call her the next day.

In the vehicle, Laura quizzed Lt. Klink as to what he thought of Charlene. He gave evasive answers, but both George and she could tell that he was enamored with her. The rest of the trip back to the base was quiet except for an occasional mention of George's or Laura's parents.

Lt. Klink dropped the Lees off at their quarters then headed back to pick up Charlene so that they could spend some quiet time together. She was waiting for him outside the hotel. She smiled at him as she hopped in. Mom Lee watched as they drove away.

She looked over at Dad Lee and said, "Paul, Charlene just left with that nice Lieutenant Klink. Maybe there's hope for her after all."

"Sally, don't worry about her," Paul said. "She is young and full of pep. Come on over here and let's get some rest." Sally walked over and got into bed and gave Paul a kiss. "Good night."

# A Short Reunion

As George and Laura got up the next morning, they saw a much different-looking sky than they had seen the day before. They took the elevator down to the lobby where Lt. Klink was reading the paper. He spotted them, put it down, stood, and greeted them, "Good morning, Major and Mrs. Lee."

They returned it. "Good morning."

Then the lieutenant asked, "Do you know that we are under hurricane warnings?"

Laura looked at George. "No, we had no idea. Do you think we should go meet with our parents?"

"I think maybe we are still permitted to be on the roads," Lt. Klink replied. "So we could possibly make it over there if we hurry."

George said, "All right, we will go right now, if you can."

Lt. Klink turned and headed out to get the car. It didn't take long to get to the relatives' hotel. As they got out of the vehicle, Charlene came over and got in the front seat.

"I'll go with you as you park the car, if it's all right."

Lt. Klink smiled broadly as Laura gave a knowing look at George.

"We'll see you over at the restaurant after we get our parents," George said. "Take your time, Lieutenant. Just watch her. She just might cast her spell on you."

"Sir, I think she already has," Klink returned. The rain came in earnest as they drove off to park.

Inside the lobby, George asked for the room numbers of their parents. They knocked on the door of Laura's parents and heard her mom ask her dad to answer the door. He greeted them and invited them in and just happened to look down the hallway and asked, "Why is the sky so dark?"

Laura answered, "We are under hurricane warnings, Dad."

Mom came into the room. "Really, we haven't seen the news. We were so tired that we went straight to bed last night."

George's mom stuck her head out of their room and cried, "I wondered what the ruckus was all about. Have you guys heard about the hurricane warnings? I don't think we will be flying back home today. Do you?"

Simon Krieger joined in, "I hadn't thought about that. We were just packing. Do you think we could make it over to Reagan? If not, I'll have to call work and let them know what is going on."

George had an idea. "Let me call General Murphy and see if he knows." He pulled out his cell phone, and just as he did, it rang. He answered, "Hello, Major Lee here."

It was Lt. Klink. "Sir, I just got word that if we hurry, we might get your folk on a flight from Reagan if they hurry right over before they are severely affected by this weather."

"That's good news, Lieutenant. Do you have any idea what time we are due to leave?"

"I think we can take the van. We should miss the storm," Lt. Klink said. "You and Mrs. Lee should definitely head back to your quarters and pick up your things."

George's cell phone rang. He answered, "Good morning, Major Lee here."

"Good morning, George, this is—can you believe it— General Murphy. I have arranged for you and Laura to leave this morning before the storm hits in full force, so get your things and have Lt. Klink drive you to Reagan where a military plane will be waiting. Major, I'm sorry I am not personally present to shake your hand and say good-bye, but it has been an honor to make your acquaintance and I wish you God's speed. Perhaps we will serve together again. I haven't been reassigned so I am not sure what the future holds yet. If Laura is close by, I'd like to say good-bye to her if I may."

"Sure thing, but before I hand the phone over to her, I want to express my deepest respect and admiration to you, sir," George said. "Thanks for all your beneficent kindness and directions. Without your leadership, the project would not have been completed so quickly. Good-bye and thanks again, now here's Laura."

As Laura answered the general, George apprised Lt. Klink of what Murphy had told him. "As soon as you finish your breakfast, we had better go get our things."

"Yes, sir. I am about finished," Klink said.

Charlene said, "Since we are going to the same airport, I'll ride with you guys. I've got my things packed, so I shouldn't hold you up."

George smiled. "Aren't you going with Mom and Dad? I thought you would want to ride with them."

"Come on, George," Charlene said with a slightly reddened face. "I like the way Lt. Klink drives."

"I think you like more than his driving, sis," George joked, "but I think it will be okay, so go get your things. That is if it's okay with Lt. Klink. What do you say, Lieutenant?"

Lt. Klink smiled as he answered, "As you warned, she's cast her spell on me, so how can I refuse."

Charlene lightly elbowed Lt. Klink in the ribs. "Oh, you two, stop it."

The rain had let up a bit as they hurriedly finished their meals and George, Laura, and Charlene headed toward the front to wait on Lt. Klink to bring the car. Their parents hugged them as Charlene retrieved her bags from her room and checked out. Lt. Klink helped place her things in the trunk and then they left.

It didn't take long for George and Laura to pack up things at their quarters. They went by the front desk and informed the attendant that they were leaving and thanked him for a comfortable stay. The attendant wished them well and said that he hoped to see them again when they returned. George and Laura rushed outside where the staff car waited. Lt. Klink assisted with loading their bags and soon they were headed for Reagan and their flights. George and Laura talked about what his next assignment might be, where they would spend their honeymoon, and how glad they would be to see their comrades again.

"I'll be happy to see Harry, Lt. Dewitt, and the rest of the soldiers and give them news of their promotions. That should make life a bit easier for them," George told her.

The rain had let up once again, and temporarily, the sky was just overcast with dark clouds. They arrived at the airport in about forty-five minutes. Over the past few days, they had been living a dream and time had just flown by. Inside the airport, the families were escorted to the appropriate airline gates and checked their bags.

The van driver said, "Excuse me, but I'd better get back before the storm hits." Before he left, he walked over to Major Lee, shook his hand and told him, "Major Lee, I just want to thank you for what you have done for our country. God bless you both in your future endeavors." He saluted him and shook hands with Laura before he turned to walk away.

Fortunately, everyone was going through Atlanta, so George and Laura could get to know their in-laws better. From there, they would take different planes to their respective destinations. Lt. Klink delivered George's and Laura's luggage to the military plane. He told George that it was scheduled to take off near the same time as their families. Charlene hung around Lt. Klink like she had known him all her life.

Laura commented, "Isn't that a beautiful sight?"

"They kind of remind me of ourselves when we first met," George replied.

The family sat facing each other as they waited for the time to board their flights. Lt. Klink's phone rang. He stood and hurried over to George.

"Sir, they just informed me that you and Mrs. Lee should hurry to your plane. I'm sorry, but it's some kind of emergency that requires you to leave immediately."

George and Laura jumped to their feet and apologized to their parents for having to leave unexpectedly. Almost in one breath, the Lees said, "Not again."

Then Mom asked, "When will we see you two again?"

George answered, "Dad, Mom, I don't really know. I have no idea what's happening. I love you. We'll try to see you soon."

Laura hugged them as George explained to her parents what had happened. Laura and he gave them all hugs and they hurried off with Lt. Klink with Charlene tagging along. They walked through the airport past security personnel toward the waiting plane.

George turned to Lt. Klink and shook his hand, "Lieutenant Klink, thank you for all your help over the past few days. More than likely, we may see you again, the way my sister seems to be taken by your charms."

Klink smiled, came to attention, and saluted Major Lee. "I enjoyed every moment of it, especially since we brought Charlene."

Charlene came up and gave George and Laura hugs. "I love you guys and wish you the best. I do hope nothing serious is happening and that I will see you two soon. Bye."

As they climbed the ramp to the plane, they waved their good-byes. They looked toward the terminal and saw their parents waving too.

As soon as they were seated, the copilot came back and greeted them. He returned to the pilot's seat and the engines revved a bit as they headed for the runway. Soon, they were cruising above the clouds at about 35,000 feet. They could see the shoreline of the Gulf of Mexico between the billowing dark clouds just to the southeast. It seemed like no time until they were crossing the Rocky Mountain Range. A short time afterward, the pilot announced that they would soon begin their descent. The plane tilted and started its landing approach. The landing flaps lowered on the wings and the landing gear jarred the plane as they locked down. Soon, they could see the landing strip ahead. George thought about how glad he would be to see Harry and Lt. Dewitt. It didn't take but a few minutes to retrieve their luggage and head for the local National Guard Armory where the military under Dewitt's command awaited reassignment orders and leave papers. The civilians among them had been debriefed and were waiting for release to their homes and families or perhaps another assignment.

A hush fell over what was once a din of hundreds of conversations when Laura and George entered the building. Lt. Dewitt and Sgt. Collins immediately walked over to Major Lee, stood at attention, and saluted him.

Harry looked at his insignia and said, "Welcome back and congratulations, Major Lee."

George almost hugged Harry, he was so glad to see him.

"Good afternoon, Sergeant," George said. "It's good to see you and Patrick. Can you guys have some sort of PA set up so that I may speak to everyone? I have a very important announcement to make."

Lt. Dewitt said, "Yes, sir. It's good to see you too, Major, and I too say congratulations on your promotion. We heard the scuttlebutt about you and Colonel Murphy receiving the Medal of Honor." He looked over at Laura. "What about this young lady receiving a Medal of Service, a new medal designed by the president just for her. Congratulations."

Everyone shook hands as the crowd gathered closer.

Lt. Dewitt informed George that a crew had been working on it and had indicated that it was nearly ready. George thanked him, walked over to a desk, and stood on it.

"Hey, everyone, let me have your attention. I requested that I might come back to say my good-byes again. I left so abruptly that I had very little time before. I am so proud to have been associated with men and women with such work ethic and integrity as you folk. Thank you for your efforts that have actually resulted in averting what most likely would have been WWIII. I am privileged to announce that because of our achievements, every civilian on any team will receive a substantial bonus of 30 percent of your annual salary. For each of you military personnel involved in this project, you will receive a promotion of one rank. For example, if you are a private, you will be promoted to PFC. Sgt. Decker is now a first sergeant. Sgt. Collins has been promoted to the rank of 2nd Lt. Collins, and First Lt. Dewitt has been promoted to the rank of captain. So congratulations are sent directly from the president, the now General Murphy, and me. Again, I say to each one of you, thanks for a job well done."

"At the conclusion of this meeting, civilian personnel may gather their things, wait to board buses that will take you to the airport and flights for home. Good-bye to you all, and may God bless and prosper you with His best blessings."

After George dismissed everyone, pandemonium set in as the crowd congratulated one another about their good fortune. First Sgt. Decker stuck his head out of a door as George was explaining the ranks and finally got through the crowd to Laura and gave her a hug.

"What about our singing career, beautiful?"

They had a big laugh as George congratulated him.

"Congratulations on your promotion, Major Lee," Decker continued. "You deserve it. I didn't know General Murphy, but we heard you two got Medals of Honor, though. It's a miracle that we were able to get the project done so quickly. Just think, because you guys did all the work, I get a promotion. That's the government I work for. They take care of their own".

George and Laura decided to stick around and have one last meal with the group. It was nice to sit at a table with Captain Dewitt who still had first lieutenant bars on. There were also 2nd Lt. Collins, and 1st Sgt. Decker. George reminded Dewitt that he needed to get those captain bars on.

"Oh, by the way, I think I may have met your wife at an Air Force PX."

Dewitt asked, "Was her name Kara?"

George answered, "Why, yes it was. She sent her love."

Dewitt got excited. "Was she okay?" George nodded in the affirmative. "Thank you, Major Lee. About the insignia,

I think they have an Army surplus store down the street so I'll pick them up after we finish up here."

The others around the table said that they would do the same. Near the end of the meal, a staff sergeant came to the table with a phone and told Major Lee that he had a phone call.

George stood, took the phone, walked into a quiet room, and answered, "Major Lee here."

George heard a familiar voice speak, "Hello, Major Lee. I hope you had a nice flight and are having a good time with your former command."

"Yes, I did, General Murphy," George answered, "and we're having a meal with them as we speak, sir."

General Murphy continued, "George, the reason I'm calling is that I have been given the assignment to form a Special Ops Unit and I would like you to serve as their division commander. Of course, you can take the month off to have your well-deserved honeymoon and a visit with your families. As far as the new unit, you may use the same personnel you had back on the island. This location will not be so isolated and nor top secret. What do you think?"

"Sir," George answered, "I am certainly honored, but could you let me get back to you with an answer?"

"George, take all the time you need, but I think this would be a good career move for you, and I understand that Laura would have employment opportunities close to the new base," General Murphy encouraged. He gave George a phone number to get in touch with him after he and Laura made their decision.

George returned to the table and handed the phone to the staff sergeant and thanked him for its use. He asked Laura to come speak with him in private. They walked over to a room that contained a desk and couple of chairs. He told Laura what General Murphy had offered him and the potential for jobs for her near the camp.

"Honey, I told him that I would give him an answer after I talked with you. He said that we would have a month for our honeymoon and the visits with our families. What do you think?"

Laura thought a few minutes. "I'm unsure. It sounds like it's something that's manageable. After all, we have to make our livelihood some way. If you want to keep the same military personnel that we had on the island, why not ask them if that would be okay with them."

George said, "Sounds great. I think that when they know they can have their families with them, the majority will agree, so let's go break the news to the men at our table."

As George and Laura returned to the table, the men were about to get up and leave, but George asked them to hold up for a bit. "Gentlemen, that phone call was from General Murphy. He informed me that he wanted me to head up a Special Ops Division. Would you gentlemen consider serving with me in that unit? Everyone would be able to have their families with them, and there would not be the isolation and top secret requirements on the island. I told the general that I would get back with him with my answer. If you are willing, I will offer the same opportunity to all the military personnel that served with us on the island, otherwise, I am not sure I will take position."

Captain Dewitt asked, "Does that mean that Lt. Collins and First Sgt. Decker will be working with us. How about Master Sergeant Allen Grant, could he still be the mess sergeant?"

"I think that would work if he is willing," George agreed. They all stood and reached for the major's hand, and with one voice, they agreed, "I'll do it."

George looked at Laura who was smiling and shaking her head yes at him. "Captain Dewitt, could you get all the military people together so we can ask them if they want to join us? And I will need that PA set again."

"Yes, sir," Captain Dewitt answered, "I'll get that PA going again."

George and Laura talked about their honeymoon plans as they waited. Soon, they heard Captain Dewitt's voice over the PA, requesting that all military personnel gather around for some exciting news.

Laura said, "George, while you are in that meeting, I'm going to look up Mary and talk with her if she hasn't already gone."

George agreed. "Tell her I said hello."

He headed for the desk he had used as a speaker's platform before. When it looked as though everyone had gathered around, Captain Dewitt asked, "Does anyone know of anybody that is absent?"

A PFC answered, "Sir, Specialist Pruett is in the latrine, sir."

Laughter broke out among the troops as Dewitt smiled and said, "Thanks for that info. Will you catch him up on what transpires here when he gets here, Private?"

"Yes, sir, I will. Oh, there he is now, sir."

Dewitt continued, "Good! I think you all will be interested in what Major Lee's proposal, so gather in close. Captain, excuse me, I mean, Major Lee, they're all yours."

George stepped upon the desk and took the microphone and said, "Thank you, Private Dewitt." There was a roar of laughter. When the laughter subsided, George said, "Just kidding, Captain. Ladies and gentlemen, the reason you are back in here is because I have an opportunity for you. You have a chance to serve with Captain Dewitt, 2nd Lt. Collins, and Sergeants Decker and Grant and me in roles far less secretive than your last assignment. Your families will be with you on base. It will be a Special Ops Unit. I'm not quite sure of all the details yet, but some of you will be assigned to help set up the new camp. I will join you in about a month so we can begin training together in earnest. This is offered strictly on a voluntary basis. Your promotions will be in effect whether or not you volunteer, so either way you will enjoy the raises that accompany the promotions. You will be able to keep your families on base, but most of all, you will be working with people whom you already know. Let me see a show a show of hands of those who are interested in continuing to work with us."

George waited for what seemed like a long time, yet there was no response. The sergeants stood and motioned for everyone to raise their hands. At first, a few hands were seen and then George asked, "Are there any questions before we leave?"

One staff sergeant yelled, "Will we be able to see our families every night or will we be away from them for weeks?"

George replied, "Sergeant, your family will be in quarters on the base, and with normal exceptions, you should be able to be with them most every night unless you are posted for guard duty or some other assignment. The duties will be similar to those in other units. Does that answer your question?"

"Yes, sir, thank you," the sergeant said as he lifted his hands as a volunteer.

George looked over the group. "Are there any more questions? I see no hands raised, so let's try this again. I will be happy to serve with you and hope that you feel the same about me and these men beside me." Several more hands were lifted, but not enough to satisfy George. "That's better, but it's not enough for me to tell General Murphy that I will command the unit. It looks as though many of you would rather serve under different leaders whom you do not know. Those who would rather do that please excuse yourselves at this time and leave the room. It is my understanding that you will be given a week's furlough beginning today. Remember, if you should just happen to change your minds before you go to your assignment, you are welcome to give Captain Dewitt a call. Meanwhile, those who are volunteering, give him your names and contact information so you can be contacted you about where to report for the new assignment with our new unit. Perhaps you need to contact a loved one and discuss things with them. Just make sure Captain Dewitt knows about it before you go to another assignment.

"Let me remind you, you will have two options. One, you may remain under my command. Captain Dewitt, Lt. Collins, and other NCOs have chosen to stay with me. You may pick up these orders from Lt. Collins. Option number 2: You may pick up orders that Captain Dewitt has. Please think about your choices before you pick up your paperwork. I reiterate, see Lt. Collins to stay with us, or see Lt. Dewitt to pick up paperwork for another assignment. I would be thrilled to have you remain with us, but the decision is entirely yours to make.

"Just a reminder, make sure you get those rank patches sewed on ASAP. You can pick up insignia at your duty station."

Lt. Collins stood and commanded, "Attention," as Major Lee turned to leave the microphone. Captain Dewitt headed for a room as Lt. Collins instructed everyone who wanted to join the newly formed unit to follow Captain Dewitt to the table and give him the necessary information. A few went to see Sgt. Decker. Several soldiers remained undecided.

George stood at a vantage point where he could observe the line formed to sign up to go with his new unit. He was amazed to see that all of the women soldiers decided to stick with their comrades. George watched a while then decided to find Laura before contacting General Murphy as he had promised. He spotted her still talking with Mary. Several other women were gathered around happily talking. As George watched, he thought over the last few days he had spent with that lovely lady and felt that he truly was one of the luckiest men in the world. Her smile and wit showed as she talked with Mary and other friends she had made on the island.

They all grew silent as he approached. They greeted him and then began to scatter. Mary hung around a little while to say hello. She smiled and gave George a warm hug.

"It's good to see that you are taking care of Laura. Wow! Major Lee. Congratulations!"

"Hi, Mary," George said, "I'm sorry to interrupt, but I must confab with this beautiful lady in private for a moment. Would you please excuse us for a bit?"

They walked some distance from the others where George told her his disappointment about so few volunteering for the new unit.

Laura consoled him, "George, honey, I can see why you are disappointed, but I can also see their point of view. After all, they spent three weeks totally isolated from the world outside the island. That was rough. Some more may come around before the deadline. Have you called General Murphy yet?"

George pulled out his cell phone and dialed Murphy's number and told him that he accepted his offer, but that he was disappointed in the number who stayed with them.

Murphy said, "Now, George, more will decide to stick with us, so don't be discouraged. You should be pleased that the men closest to you have decided to hang with you. This will be a great unit. You'll see, son. Perhaps you and Laura had better pray about this before you take off on that well-deserved honeymoon. By the way, my wife Gloria and I have sent you a belated wedding present. It should be arriving any minute now. We will see you guys in a month. God bless you two real good. Give my regards to those men and women who are sticking with you in the new unit."

George agreed and then the conversation ended. He headed over to the sign-up line and told his crew that the general had sent his regards.

"Ladies and gentlemen, General Murphy sends his regards. I think I will be leaving in a few minutes. So I will leave all this in the capable hands of Captain Dewitt," George informed them.

As he was turning to leave, Lieutenant Klink met him with a sharp salute. "Major Lee, I have something for you and your wife. General Murphy wanted Laura to be present when you receive these present from his wife and him."

George returned the salute and said, "It's good to see you, Lt. Klink. Follow me and we will find her."

Laura was still talking with Mary and some others who had rejoined them when George and Lt. Klink found her. "Laura, General Murphy and his wife has sent us a present, and he wanted us to be together when we received it."

Laura ran over to Lt. Klink and gave him a slight hug. "Hello, Lieutenant Klink, I didn't expect to see you this soon."

Klink answered, "I didn't expect to see you either, but I am happy to deliver your gift from General and Mrs. Murphy." He reached inside the breast pocked of his dress blues jacket and pulled out two envelopes. He handed one to each of them.

George pulled a small knife out of his pocked and opened his envelope and then opened Laura's for her and handed it back. They both pulled out the contents of their envelopes slowly. Laura broke into tears.

"No way! George, these are reservations for a fancy hotel in Honolulu, Hawaii. Let me see yours." Her eyes widened further. "Hey, everyone, George and I are going to Hawaii for our honeymoon. The Murphys sent us airline tickets and hotel reservations."

Cheers rang out as she reached over and kissed George, and several ladies cheered and clapped and came over and gave Laura hugs.

They thanked Lt. Klink for delivering the gifts. Lt. Klink said with a big smile, "Folk, I meant, sir, please look at the tickets and you will see that we need to be at the airport within a few minutes in order for you to catch your flight. So we had better get started pretty soon, don't you think?"

They agreed, and Laura went after their things with Lt. Klink in tow. George headed over to say his good-byes to Harry, Dewitt, and Sgt. Decker who were talking with other soldiers when George approached. He found them in a huddle. They turned and saluted as George approached.

"I just wanted to let you know that we must be going now. I just want to say good-bye to my friends. Harry, when you see Pam and Tommy, give them hugs for me. Captain Dewitt, say hello to your wife when you see her. Sgt. Decker, keep practicing, you may still be able to get a quartet together at the new base. For now, General Murphy has given Laura and me tickets to and hotel reservations in Honolulu, and we need to leave immediately to catch the plane. God bless you, men. I will see you in about a month. You all have my cell phone number, so don't hesitate to call and say, hello. See you later, my friends."

He shook hands with them left to find Lt. Klink and Laura. Several stood near the exit waving good-bye as they loaded into a staff car and headed toward the airport.

# The Honeymoon

The flight was long and tiring, so they were happy when they saw Oahu and the Honolulu International Airport as the plane descended and aligned with the runway on its approach.

"Finally, my love, we are able to celebrate the most momentous day of our lives," George said. "I love you and surely do hope that we can have a break from stress for a few days."

They exited the plane through the ramp that extended form the terminal. Beautiful smiling black-haired Hawaiian girls welcomed them with traditional leis that they hung around their necks. Their warm greetings made them feel good about getting there. They picked up their luggage and headed for the car rental booths. They rented a smaller

SUV because of its fuel economy; gas was quite expensive here. They asked directions to the resort and went straight there and checked in.

Liquid sunshine, Hawaii's term for rain, was designed by someone to make it not feel as wet when you get rained on, began falling moments after they got to their rooms. They lay down for a short rest, but the nap turned out to be much longer than they planned. It was dark when Laura awakened. George also stirred and looked over and gave her an amorous look. She reciprocated and moved closer, so dinner was delayed.

The atmosphere of the dining room was cheery as they were led to a table. The liquid sunshine had stopped as the clouds moved away from the island. Dinner was pleasant as they talked and perused the island's tourist attractions. They decided to drive up to see the Blow Hole the next morning.

After seeing the Blow Hole George was disappointed. Its spray was produced by ocean waves splashing against rocks underneath an overhanging rock ledge. The water forced up through a hole in the ledge appeared as mist of an exhaling whale. It was interesting sight, but because he had never seen a whale exhale, he was unsure if it really looked anything like a whale exhaling. They lingered a while, sipping their iced tea. As they walked back to the parking area, they decided to drive up to the North Beach and watch surfers ride the waves. They stopped to eat hotdogs and french fries at burger joint in Miliani.

Laura remarked, "Probably not the healthiest, but it sure does taste good."

George agreed as he took a big hunk out of the end of his dog.

The waves were high, and as he was looking at the water, he was reminded of the waves he saw as he was being transferred to the air craft carrier a few days earlier. These waves were a lot more relaxing than those. He mentioned his thoughts to Laura who said that she was thinking of the very same thing.

"You are having a bad influence on me. We are already having similar thoughts."

George reached over and gave her a hug, and after checking to see if no one was watching, he gave her a kiss.

"Oh, George, this is so relaxing. I have enjoyed every minute of our trip so far," she whispered.

"I know, dear, me too," George said. "It's been the most relaxing time since I played with the kid goats back on the farm."

Laura laughed. "Maybe you can find a couple dolphins to play with out here."

"I couldn't grab them by the horns," George laughed as he spoke.

There was a park nearby so they drove over to see what it was like. The park bordered both sides of a valley stream that began at a waterfalls. There were white peacocks roaming freely as they showed off their beautiful tail feathers. Other birds, a pot-bellied pig, a llama, and others not native to the islands were seen. Laura was getting a bit tired so they decided that it was time to head back to their room. As they headed south, on H201, they caught the smell of smoke from harvested sugar cane fields being burned. They saw vast pineapple fields owned by a name brand canning company.

"I have had many pineapples, but had no idea that they were grown in such large fields," George said.

Laura said, "And what about all that used cane stalks being burned? When we get back to the room, let's call our parents."

"Don't forget that there is a nine-hour time difference between us and them," George reminded Laura.

She added the time difference in her head and said, "I think it should be okay. Let's try it. It should be about 8:00 a.m. there now, and about 11:00 at your parents' place. I think it should be okay."

"All right, let's do that," George said as they headed into Honolulu. They entered the hotel lobby and George noticed Laura's nose was getting quite red. "Wow, you are getting a burn. You are going to be as tanned as one of the Hawaiian hula girls if you keep outside enough. Of course, you will have to dye your hair to really look like one. And you will have to get one of those grass skirts."

"Those girls have such beautiful skin, so I think that would be nice," Laura answered. "Don't you, George?"

He looked thoughtful. "I might not know who I was waking up beside." He hesitated and then laughingly said, "I was just joking. Let's eat before we call our parents. What do you say?"

"Sure, I'm starved," Laura responded as they headed toward the hotel restaurant. The meal was delicious, and they enjoyed talking with one another.

When the meal ended, they headed for their room and called their parents. After they finished the phone calls, Laura walked into the bedroom area and yelled, "Hey, George, come in here. Please hurry!"

George asked, "What's wrong, honey?" as he entered the room and immediately saw the problem. "Man, someone has gone through our things. We had better call hotel security."

It didn't take long for security to get there. The manager was called, and after he understood the situation, he apologized, "Mr. and Mrs. Lee, we have insurance that will cover any losses you may have sustained. Just let us know what you are missing, and we will reimburse you for their replacement costs. I am so sorry this has happened. This is the first time something like this has ever happened here."

"It really doesn't look like much, if anything at all, was taken," Laura told the manager.

After a bit, the manager excused himself and started to leave. George walked into the hall with him and asked him if he could have a word with him. He stopped and agreed, "Surely. What can I do for you?"

"Well, sir," George began, "I was wondering if your security has the means to check to see if the room is bugged. If so, could you have them check to see if that is the case in our room?"

The manager looked surprised. "Yes, we do, but it would be highly unusual for something like that to happen here, especially for honeymooners, sir."

"It's true that we are on our honeymoon, but I am a major in the armed forces and have just completed a very important mission," George stated. "So there possibly may be some connection with this break in and that mission. It is highly unlikely, but I can't afford to take any chances."

"What kind of mission, if I may ask?" the manager asked.

George got that look. "I'm sorry, but I am not at liberty to discuss it with anyone. It did involve matters of national security."

"I see. We will get on that right away, sir," he said as he stuck his head in the door and motioned for the head of security to come into the hallway. He instructed him to discreetly run a sweep of the room and report to him what was found. The security employee headed off to get the equipment.

After the other security personnel had gone, George helped him search the room for hidden listening devices or surveillance equipment. The scanner indicated that there was a bug in the room. It got louder as they swung it toward the light shade. He removed it carefully with tissue.

"It probably will have no fingerprints, but it may be worth checking it out. One more thing, don't say anything to my wife about this. There is no need to worry her any further."

The security head agreed. George said, "Just to make sure, before you go, let's check the phone handsets and make sure they are clean."

George located another listening device out of the phone's mouthpiece.

"I'll get these to a friend of mind in the police department, and he will check them out for us. It will take a couple days, so be patient, sir. Could I ask you a question? Have you had some experience with things like this before?"

"I'm sorry, I am not allowed to discuss anything about my past assignments with anyone, but I've heard of such things as this," George said. "Thanks for doing this."

The manager soon came with a small crew to help the Lees move to another room. It didn't take long until George and Laura were alone once again, with many apologies from the management, and a promise that he would do his best to prevent this from recurring.

It took a while for Laura to calm down, but finally, she calmed down enough to be able to rest.

The next morning as they were going for breakfast, the security chief waved him over. He told Laura, "Honey why don't you go find us a table and I'll be in there in a little while."

She agreed and George went to meet with the security guy.

"Hello, Major Lee, after I contacted my friend at the PD, he found out through some military contact that you just might be the national hero which President Whinton recently presented the Medal of Honor. He also found a print on one of the listening devices." He grabbed George's hand, shook it, and continued, "It is an honor to have you staying with us, sir. I talked with the manager and all your meals will be on the house because of your service to our nation."

George warned, "I see from your name tag that your name is John. John, please limit this information to those whom already have it. Just to let you know, the CIA will be checking with this hotel to see if any information about my recent mission has been discussed. I appreciate your support, but please keep this information and this discussion to yourself. When you learn who the fingerprint belongs to, please let me know."

"Major Lee, if I receive any news, I will let you know immediately," John promised. "Now, go and have a nice breakfast with your lovely wife. And congratulations on your recent marriage, sir."

"Thank you, John," George said as they shook hands and turned to meet his waiting bride.

Breakfast was delicious, especially the tasty rolls. Laura thought was some of the best tasting rolls she had ever tasted. George agreed.

"They are good, but my mother just might change your mind about it being the best because she makes some of the best most fattening homemade rolls you could ever eat."

"When we visit, I'll have to try some," Laura answered.

They decided just to tour Honolulu that day. They saw some of the largest ships either of them had ever seen, even larger than the ones they were aboard after leaving the island. They talked about owning a yacht like the one docked nearby.

Lunch was delicious and they got more exercise that day than they had gotten since they left the island. After they finished eating, they visited a few shops. George spotted a purse that he thought Laura might like.

"Hey, babe, look at that purse and those matching shoes. Why don't you try on the shoes and get that purse to match."

It didn't take George long to convince her to try on the shoes. She purchased them and the purse, but George was not finished.

"How about that beautiful red and black dress; wouldn't that look great with the purse and shoes?"

She smiled. "George, are you sure? That looks awfully expensive."

Once again, she was easily convinced that she should at least see how it looked on her. George couldn't believe his eyes when she came out of the dressing room.

"Wow! Would you look at that? I am going to send Mom and Dad a picture of this beauty."

She blushed as she walked over to a mirror and looked at herself. "My, it is a beautiful outfit. Everything matches so well. But, George, it's so expensive. Can we afford it?"

He grinned. "We'll take it out of your bonus. I like it." He turned to the saleslady. "We'll take the outfit. Please wrap it for us. Thank you."

Laura quickly changed back into the clothes that she had worn all day. It took about fifteen minutes for the outfit to be wrapped, so they browsed until it was ready.

As they walked the few blocks to their hotel, Laura commented that the stars look different here.

"Well you are used to seeing them from the north side of the equator, but you are south of it now, so the stars do appear different."

Laura commented, "They're still a beautiful part of God's creation, aren't they? Oh, George, I'm so happy, you have made me one of the happiest girls in the world, and I love you so much."

"And you, my dear, have made me the happiest man in the world," George returned as he stopped, faced her, and drew her to himself. They embrace and kissed. Some people stopped and clapped as the two prolonged their kiss. They broke off the kiss, a bit embarrassed. George, however, bowed a deep bow and that brought further clapping. He waved, took Laura's hand, and they continued their walk toward the hotel.

Laura tried on the dress again before they dined. "This is the most beautiful dress I have ever owned. It is so beautiful."

George interrupted, "Do you know what makes it so beautiful? It is the lady inside it that gives it that special form and makes it look so great."

Laura ran over to him and grabbed him. "This time there won't be any clapping." She gave him a big smooch as they embraced. At dinner, she got several comments about her beautiful outfit.

On their way to breakfast the next morning, George felt relaxed, but all the while, he was alert for any sign of something that did not fit. It seemed as though everything was normal, so he was relieved and happy about that.

As Laura and he were being seated, he saw a familiar face. He took a second and immediately recognized him as Amos Farrago, the spy who had escaped from the island. He excused himself and walked over to where he was sitting and calmly said, "Hello, Mr. Farrago, How have you been?"

Amos Farrago answered, "I've been doing well and keeping very busy making sure that nothing happens to you or your family, Major Lee."

"I'm glad you are well, but did you know that someone planted a couple bugs in our room?" George asked.

"I was in there just before you got back from your shopping trip," Farrago said, "but I couldn't find them. What tipped you off that they were there?"

"Well, you left a mess, so I had hotel security check the room with a bug scanner and they found two," George said. "I had better get back over to Laura before she gets too curious."

"Before you go," Farrago said as he stood, "thank you and your team for building that device so quickly and destroying that apocalyptic device those terrorists were planning to deploy. I believe you saved my family from an awful death. Thank you again."

They shook hands, and before George turned to leave, he told him, "I'll be in contact again."

He returned to the table, and Laura told him, "I took the liberty of ordering you coffee. They'll take our order when they bring our drinks. Who was that man you were talking with?"

George was forming an answer when the waitress brought the drinks. They ordered their food and talked as they waited for the food. George was relieved that during their conversation, Laura had forgotten that she had asked about the man he had talked with. The meal was pleasant as they continued to talk about what they were going to do that day.

"Why don't we stick around here again today and go down to the beach?"

George said, "I'm afraid I might see too many near-naked women and we'd have to hurry back up here."

Laura gave George a warning look, so he said, "Really, I'm not comfortable on the beach, and I think the swimming suits really are too revealing. If you want to go, I'll find something else to do while you are gone."

"Okay, if you want to be a prude," Laura said with a smile. "I'll just sit near the beach with a pop and watch for a little while."

George kissed Laura as she left the room. In a little while, he decided to walk to a gun shop he remembered from the day before. He looked over some weapons, but he knew that if he purchased one, he would never be able to take it out of the state. He just liked to see how they worked. Weapons had always interested him. In fact, he taught weapons classes at the military academy as a second lieutenant. He became aware that someone was standing beside him. A familiar voice spoke, "Nice, aren't they, George."

He turned, and sure enough, it was Farrago. "Man, you really are good. I didn't hear the door sound when you entered."

"I've had a lot of practice sneaking up on people, George," Farrago said. "How did you ever manage to be alone? Let's go somewhere so we can talk and not have the chance of being videoed. Wait for me at the corner."

Farrago left and George exited the store, turned right, and walked to the corner. He waited for a couple minutes, then Farrago pulled up and motioned for him to get in the car. They drove a couple blocks turned left, then right at the next block and drove down an alley. When Farrago felt confident they were not being followed, he headed into a grocery store parking lot where lots of cars were parked. He pulled between two vans. He opened the console between the seats and pulled out a .357 Colt and handed it to George.

"You had better hang on to this because I think espionage agents have located you and Laura."

"Is that who planted the bugs?" George asked. "I thought they had assumed I was dead."

Farrago answered, "They did, but there is a mole at the White House, George."

George asked, "Do you know who he is?"

Farrago shook his head. "No, but he is deep in the system. Perhaps even the vice president."

George stuck the revolver into his belt and pulled his shirttail out to cover it. "You're kidding me! How could they get that deep? Everyone is checkout by the FBI before they are permitted to run for office."

"I'm not sure, but they are top-notch in their skills," Farrago responded, "and once you are in, you have to do something pretty stupid to be found out. Here is a box of shells just in case."

"Thanks. So they probably know who I am," George told Farrago. "The hotel security manager said that a police friend told him that he knew I had just received the Medal of Honor."

"Man, this is serious," Farrago said with a concerned look, "I think we had better get you out of that hotel into a safer place. When I drop you off, you head for your room and pack things up and I'll help you get it to the car. When Laura gets back, tell her that you have found a safer, nicer place and get her to the car and follow me. There is a safer place for you guys."

They headed back and had most of it out to Farrago's car when Laura walked in.

"George, what's going on? What are you doing? Why are you packing?"

George said, "Steady, honey! This is Amos Farrago. Back on the island, he helped us to fool the enemy into thinking they had succeeded in destroying the facility and killing everyone there. There are things happening that require us leave right away."

Laura thought about the break-in and saw how dead serious George was. She immediately began helping them load the rest of the things. When they were done, they got into their rental car. On their way, George had Laura contact General Murphy and informed him about what was happening. She gave the phone to George who warned him that there was a mole in the White House who was close to the president and that he had informed someone that Laura and he were in Hawaii. He also told him that hotel security knew he had just received the Medal of Honor, and that he was following Farrago to a safer location.

Murphy thanked George and warned him, "Be very careful and don't take any chances. This sounds seriously dangerous."

After making several switch backs, Farrago drove them to the dead end of one of the roadways and parked near a well-camouflaged motorcycle. Laura riding behind him was surprised to see a cabin hidden from view on the road by trees. It was about three hundred yards the other side of a small stream. He returned and shuttled their things to the cabin. George and Farrago entered cabin where Laura was waiting.

"This is nice," Laura commented. "I could live in a place like this."

Farrago smiled. "Thanks, I like it. I've owned it since I had an assignment here. It's owned under the name Adam Frank."

George looked surprised. "You own this? I guess you own several places under your cover names all over the country and a few foreign ones, huh?"

"Yeah, you never know when you may need to hide out for a spell," Farrago laughed. "Make yourselves at home." He led them over to a room and told them that they could stay in it and that he would stay in the loft where he had a view of the ocean and the access road.

George and Laura gathered their things into their very comfortable room. The cabin was powered by solar energy so there was no record of its existence with the electric company. Water was piped in from a spring in the mountain behind the cabin.

"Laura, this is amazing," George said. "It wouldn't surprise me if he has an electric car hidden somewhere."

Laura agreed, "This truly is an amazing lifestyle he has here. How did you say you met him?"

George, who tried to be evasive but could not consciously lie to her because of his Christian morals, said, "Well, you remember when we caught the image of a spy on camera, the one that watched us test the device, well, that was Amos Farrago. After he was captured, he helped us set up the explosions that were designed to convince the enemy that we all had been killed. I decided that he should be let go."

Laura looked incredulous.

George continued, "He has family on the mainland that would have been killed if the enemy had been able to successfully employ their device. That's the reason he helped us."

"Do you mean that he was working for the enemy?" Laura asked. "How can you trust him?"

"I'll have to admit that I had deep reservations, but he has proven his loyalty by watching out for us ever since we have been off the island. He even told me that about a mole among the White House staff. He didn't know who he is, but Murphy has been informed about him. I think he has proven himself, especially if all this pans out. He was the one who messed up our room when he was looking for the bugs. He didn't find any because he heard us coming. The security man found the bugs a little too easily and then he told me that he learned about our presidential medals from a friend at the police department. I wonder if he might have planted the bugs himself after the mole informed him about the medals. Things seemed to be a little too easy with that guy. I worry about him more than I do Farrago."

"I can see why you may think these things, George," Laura said, "but let me ask you a question, why didn't you let me in on these things?"

"Honey, I didn't want you to worry," George answered. "You were enjoying yourself too much."

"Actually, I was getting kind of bored," Laura explained, "not with you, but not being active in anything productive was driving me crazy, honey."

"Okay," George responded with a look of surprise, "I promise you that you will know immediately after I learn anything from now on."

About that time, Amos Farrago knocked on the door. When he came in, he presented both of them disguises.

"I thought that we should go eat pretty soon, but I don't think it's safe to be seen publicly as George and Laura Lee."

Laura got excited. "Wow! You are not kidding are you?"

"No, ma'am, I'm not, this is a very serious situation you are in," Amos said. "We must be super cautious if you two are to get out of here alive. Laura, do you know how to use a gun?"

Laura immediately answered, "No, I really don't like guns."

"Do you mean you helped develop a weapon that can shoot people on earth from twenty-two miles in space and you are afraid of a little old 9MM hand gun?" Farrago sounded a bit irritated. Then he asked, "How about a bit of kung fu?"

"I had a few classes when I was younger," Laura answered. "Dad wanted me to learn to protect myself against people like George, here." That broke the tension as all three laughed together.

"Good," Amos said while he was still laughing between words. "It didn't seem to work. Look where George has you. How about showing me what you learned."

They all went outside and when Laura exited, Farrago lunged at her. She feigned to the right and brought up her left knee into his stomach. He fell to the ground, hugging his belly.

"Hey, she really is good, George."

"Yeah, I know," George said with a grin, "she fights me off like that all the time."

"Seriously, she's good," Amos said. "How about you, George? Are you any good at hand-to-hand combat?"

"I'm probably not as good as Laura or you, but I have had a few occasions to use it. I had to use it once or twice in Iraq," George answered. "Maybe a few other occasions I used various methods of self-defense."

They were headed back inside when George's phone rang. "George Lee here."

"Hello, George, this is Harry," the voice answered. "I just landed at the airport and was hoping you could pick me up."

George asked, "Harry, what are you doing here?"

"General Murphy sent me over," Harry answered. "He thought you might need my help. Can you pick me up or do I need to catch a cab to the hotel?"

George looked over at Farrago who indicated that they would take about an hour. Then he told Harry, "Hey, Harry, it'll be about an hour to pick you up. Okay?"

Amos convinced George and Laura that they should turn their phones off and purchase a couple burner phones.

They put their disguises on before they left the cabin. By the time they got them on and got through traffic, it was about an hour and fifteen minutes before they arrived at the terminal. In town, Farrago stopped and switched over to the cab that he had first contacted George in. George spotted Harry waiting by his bags and walked to him.

"Harry, this is George. Don't look at me, but carry your bags over to the curb and a taxi will stop and pick you up."

Farrago drove a cab up to the curb and helped Harry load his things in the trunk. They quickly drove away after Harry had gotten in, and then they picked up George. Harry was surprised to see a strange woman next to him. He hadn't recognized George, so he was starting to get nervous.

Laura said, "Hello, Harry."

George also spoke up, "Harry, it's good that you didn't recognize Laura or me. And our driver is none other than our Amos Farrago. You remember him, don't you?"

"Hello, Amos. Hey you, guys, it's good to see that you are okay," Harry said excitedly. "You had me fooled, but why all the cloak and dagger stuff?"

"We'll catch you up after we switch vehicles," Amos told Harry as the taxi made several switch backs and then pulled into an alley where the other vehicle had been parked. On the way to the cabin, George and Laura caught up on all the news and told Harry what had been happening since they arrived in Hawaii.

Meanwhile, the security manager at the hotel had falsely reported that George and Laura had stolen several thousand dollars worth of jewelry from the hotel safe. Taking his word for it, the police officer friend simply issued an APB for their arrest.

After they arrived at the cabin, Harry shook hands with Amos like they were old friends.

"How are you doing, Farrago?"

"Hi, Harry, please just call me Amos," Farrago requested. "After all we've been through together. You know, with the long needles and the planting of the explosives and my escape from that lieutenant. What was his name? I think it was Lt. Dewitt. I felt bad for him getting into much trouble over my escape."

Harry answered, "Actually, he didn't get into any trouble at all. Our illustrious major took all the blame. Not only was he kept out of trouble, he earned a promotion to captain. General Murphy was very understanding about you, Amos."

"He sounds like man after my own heart," he said as he pulled into the parking lot of a shop that sold cell phones. "These guys are fairly reasonable on their prices. Laura, maybe you should buy three phones. Don't pay by credit card, use cash. Do you have enough cash to pay for them?"

Laura nodded and headed for the door. She returned in about ten minutes with a bag. Laura suggested that they stop at a restaurant and eat. They agreed, so they pulled over at the drive-through. Amos paid, and they sipped their to-go drinks as he headed back to the cabin. They walked together to the cabin.

"Harry, we'll go get your things after we eat."

Harry agreed and they all ate after George offered thanks to God for the food, Harry's safe arrival, and for allowing them safety during the day.

While Harry and Amos went after Harry's things, Laura and George had a little time to reflect on today's happenings.

George commented on Laura's karate expertise, "I had no idea that you could be so rough. I'm glad I didn't try anything during our long dates."

"Why do you think I wanted to get married so quickly?" Laura came back. "I knew I couldn't resist your bewitching charms."

They were still chuckling when Amos brought in the first bike load. He unloaded it and went back after another load while Harry unpacked. It wasn't long until Harry and Amos were chatting like old friends. They were talking about Afghanistan and their experiences there.

Once everything was stashed away, Amos brought out some glasses with ice and offered choices of drinks, iced tea, and several kinds of pop and other beverages. They made their choices and Amos poured their beverages and began to sing, "Praise God from whom all blessings flow." The harmony of voices praising the Father, Son, and Holy Ghost blessed them all. The atmosphere was electrified with the presence of the Holy Spirit. God's presence filled the room. Every eye was wet from tears of gladness for God's abundant mercies by the time the Doxology ended.

Harry was elated with the thought that under the direst of circumstances, God would come and bless a person in such a real and evident way.

Amos said, "I've found Christ Jesus as my personal Savior. That is the main reason I am helping you guys. I know that you folk are the real thing. I watched you on the island, and I could sense that God was blessing your work, and I knew that I could really do nothing to harm you or any of your people, Major Lee."

Suddenly, an alarm went off and Amos jumped to his feet and ran into another room. The others followed inside and saw all sorts of equipment. He switched on a monitor and saw that it was nothing but a mongoose that had tripped an alarm.

"They do that all the time, but I take no chances. The one time that I'm wrong and think it's just a mongoose and don't check it out that could be the time that I die in my sleep."

Harry looked amazed. "You have quite a setup here, Amos. There is some pretty high tech stuff. It must have cost a fortune for you to get all this equipment and set it up. Did you set it up too?"

"Yes, I purchased and installed all the equipment, including the solar power. Also, I have some other things I probably should show you. Come with me."

He led them to another room, kind of like a utility room, he reached and pushed a place in the paneling. The wall slid to one side and revealed a tunnel. He motioned for them to follow. As he entered, lights came on and the door shut behind them automatically. They walked about ten yards and came up against a stone wall. Amos walked over to the wall and placed his right hand on it and placed his left eye in front of a small hole. The wall slid aside similarly to the wall inside the cabin. They all walked inside a room filled with more instruments. TV and radio stations were available for viewing. There was even a satellite link control panel that allowed Amos to observe his cabin and the surrounding area.

Harry looked startled. "Hey, you guys look on the TV. There is a picture of you two."

Amos reached over and pressed a control button. A newscaster was reporting, "It is believed that George and Laura Lee have taken thousands of dollars worth of diamonds from the hotel safe where they had been staying. This couple should be considered armed and dangerous. If you see them, please do not approach them but call your local law enforcement emergency number."

George was flabbergasted. "Laura, I told you that I thought that security man couldn't be trusted."

Laura agreed. "It's a good thing Amos got us out of there when he did." She turned to Amos and said, "Thanks, Amos, for helping us. You did the right thing! But what do we do now?"

Harry pulled out his phone to call General Murphy to let him know what was going on, but there was no signal. Amos informed him that there was no reception from inside the mountain, but he would scramble a call to whomever he was going to contact. He pointed Harry to a phone next to a police scrambler.

"It routes calls through a satellite which relays them to the recipient." Harry dialed General Murphy's number. It rang several times before Murphy answered, "I don't recognize this number, who is this?"

"General Murphy, this is Harry Collins. You asked me to call you if anything came up. We are in a secret location with Amos Farrago. He has helped George and Laura escape dangers at the hotel, but now there is an APB out on George and Laura. They are accused of stealing jewels worth thousands from the hotel safe. And to top it all off, they are to be considered armed and dangerous. Can you do something about this fiasco, sir?"

"Harry thanks for letting me know and give Mr. Farrago my deepest appreciation for watching out for them. Tell George and Laura that I have checked on their families and they are fine. Give me a little while, and I will have the CIA take care of this hotel security man. You guys take care of yourselves. I…" The line went dead because Amos had cut the connection.

Amos explained, "I can't talk more than a minute and a half on this phone because it can be traced to the satellite link if I stay on much longer."

"That's okay," Harry said. "He said that he really appreciated you watching out for George and Laura, and he would take care of the hotel security guy."

The next morning, the TV news broadcast headlined the news that the hotel security man had been arrested for falsely reporting a theft along with several other charges, including espionage. All warrants had been canceled for George and Laura Lee who were honeymooners who had simply switched hotels.

Amos looked at them and said, "Man, your General Murphy must have a lot of clout. I don't believe I have ever seen something like this resolved so quickly. I still don't think it's safe to return to the room because the people behind this are still out there." He hesitated. "I have an idea! Hey, Harry, do you have your little kit with you? You know, the one that you used on me out on the island."

Harry answered, "I never leave home without it."

"Great," Amos said, "I think we should invite the security man to come visit us for a spell. What do you think?"

Harry agreed, "Let's do it, have you got the means to get him away from the Honolulu PD?"

"It should be a piece of cake," Amos said. "I'll take care of getting him here after breakfast, but right now, let's get some chow into our gullets."

When Laura volunteered to fix breakfast, George looked surprised. "Man, not only is she a beauty and she is tough, but she can cook too."

"Honey, you have a lot to learn about me," Laura said as she winked at him. She turned toward the kitchen as Amos went with her and showed her where the eggs, bacon, and flour were located.

After breakfast, Amos disappeared for a while, and when he returned, he really did look as though he could be a special agent for homeland security as his badge indicated. His name tag and credentials looked real too. "I'll be back in about an hour."

During that time, the trio prepared for their guest. Harry arranged his kit and George decided Laura and he would take a walk on the beach. It took a bit longer than Amos thought, but he finally arrived with the security guy blindfolded. He brought him into the room where Harry waited. Laura and George quietly left the room as Harry and Amos began to work with John.

"John, what's your real name?"

John answered, "John Adams."

"How long have you been a spy against the United States, John Adams?" Harry asked.

John looked surprised. "What do you mean a spy against the United States? Who are you guys anyway?

"Now, John, you made accusations against a couple friends of ours, and we are going to find out the reason why while you are in this room if you aren't cooperative. You may never leave this room as mobile as when you came in," Amos threatened. "You know, mobile, as in living and breathing God's good air."

John began to get a little shook up. "Do you mean I may never leave this room alive?"

"I think the statement was really quite clear," Harry said, "and I think you had better consider your future answers a bit more carefully. Let me give you a little demonstration of what you can expect if you fail to cooperate." Harry used the same two needles that he used against Amos when they first met.

John let out such a loud scream. Laura heard the sound and looked startled. George tried to convince her that Harry had inflicted no permanent damage on Amos when he questioned him back on the island and that the security man shouldn't any lasting issues either.

John was breathing heavily by now.

Harry asked him again, "How long have you been a spy, John?"

John started to say something about not being a spy and Harry plunged the pins a bit deeper into his neck.

"All right! I've been working with an Eastern cartel for about five years now. For God's sake, ease up on this torture and I'll tell you all you want to know."

Harry was relieved because he didn't really relish the idea of hurting anyone, but he knew it could be really effective if used correctly.

"See, John, how easy it is when you tell the truth. Oh, by the way, if you lie to me, I will know and things will get far worse than this. Who had you to trump up the charges against George and Laura Lee?"

"The order came down from the upper ranks," John said. "They had me plant the first bugs Lee found. I was really surprised when we got the call that their room had been broken into. I had to pretend to do my job as security head."

"Who is the man in the White House?" Harry asked.

John looked scared. "I am not really sure, but he has direct access to the president almost daily and he has a high rank in the cartel's espionage team in the United States."

"Come on, John, we already knew he was close to the president. Surely someone has said something or you've heard some brag about someone being that far up in the White House," Harry prompted.

"Well, I've heard about this guy named Prang or something like that, but I don't really know if that's his name," John said. "Now, please get these things out of my neck. Please."

"All right, I will remove them, but they will stay out only as long as you cooperate with us," Amos said. "Now are there more who are working in this area?"

They continued questioning John until Harry and Amos agreed that they had gotten all the information they could out of John.

During the questioning, George and Laura had been strolling along the beach. She had found several interesting shells as they talked about what they might do once the current crisis was over.

Harry came to meet them and informed George what they had been told. Amos went about returning the prisoner to the local authorities. Because John had been blindfolded and had earplugs in his ears during his trip to Amos's cabin, he most likely would not be able to find the cabin's location because Amos had taken several turns and twists and driven several miles on remote roads to make sure that nothing would indicate his location.

As Amos delivered John back to the city jail, none the worse for wear, John tried to inform the desk sergeant that Amos was not who he claimed to be.

He yelled, "Sergeant, this man is not..." but stopped as Farrago tightened his grip on the trigger points of his neck, still sore from where the needles had been inserted. Adams grimaced and immediately stopped talking.

The officer responded, "Yeah, right," and then thanked the disguised Farrago for bringing the man back. He also informed him that someone had been to see the prisoner. Farrago asked if he could see the visitor's register for a name. The desk sergeant showed it to him. The name read Peter Masters. Farrago asked the desk sergeant if he knew the man, but he said that he had seen him before but didn't know him. Farrago thanked him and left for the cabin. He did his usual routine of many turns, and when he felt sure that he was not being followed, he went in. His waiting guests were happy to see him and listened intently to his report.

Harry used the scrambler to call General Murphy and report what had happened. George told him thanks for removing him from the APB and getting rid of the arrest warrants.

"That's all right, George," Murphy said. "I'm sorry you had your honeymoon interrupted. We'll try to make it up to you and Laura."

"Laura was getting bored anyway, and this put a little excitement in our Hawaiian getaway," George replied.

Amos motioned that it was about time to get off, so Harry said, "Chief, we have to go now. Talk with you later, bye."

"Okay, I'll find out what I can about this Peter Masters. Call me tonight, Harry. Bye."

Amos asked his guests, "How about some Chinese takeout?"

"Hey, I'll buy if there is a place to eat it inside," George said.

It took three trips on the motorcycle to get everyone to the vehicle, and the trip to the Chinese restaurant was uneventful. They walked inside and sat down at a table for four. They all looked like a tourist who had just stopped in for a nice meal. It was an excellent meal with quiet conversation about various topics which finally turned to the subject of religion.

"Jesus Christ came to seek and to save that which was lost," Harry said, "and everyone that does not know Him is lost."

Amos asked, "How can you win people to God when you are able to torture people Harry?"

Harry answered, "That is against what I want to do, Amos. Actually, I hate doing it. I don't know if you know it or not, but those needles are actually acupuncture needles. The pain comes from striking deep into a trigger point. The pain goes away almost immediately when they are removed, but it is actually very effective in retrieving information from an unwilling prisoner, don't you think?"

"Do you mean to tell me that those things that felt like a pencil piercing my neck were only thin acupuncture needles?" Amos asked.

Harry answered, "That's right, Amos. I know they really hurt, but these are the same needles that the Chinese have used for hundreds of years to help people get well quicker. I know that it sounds like a copout, but I really do love people. That's actually why I use that technique instead a more maiming and damaging one. How long did it take you to stop feeling the effects of it?"

"I didn't think much about it until now," Amos said as he thought back. "I know the pain was gone before we left the facility to go set up the explosive charges."

"That's exactly my point, Amos," Harry said. "I do know how to inflict permanent damage, but I prefer to use acupuncture. Doctors use it in such a manner that it causes little or no pain, but our goals are not the same."

Laura tapped George on the shoulder. He turned toward her as she rolled her eyes toward the door as two Chinese men entered. Amos and Harry had observed Laura getting George's attention. Immediately, Amos looked concerned.

"That's one of the men who hired me to take care of the island facility."

George whispered, "When they are seated, let's get out of here as quietly as possible."

Instead of being seated, the men headed for a back room. As they disappeared, Amos said, "Let's go."

George paid their tab on the way out, and when they got to the car, Harry said, "This may be their headquarters. I can't believe that the very time we decided to eat Chinese, in walks a couple Chinese espionage agents."

Amos half-jokingly said, "The Lord works in mysterious ways."

George responded, "I believe God does work exactly like this. He opens doors that men through their methods could never push open."

Harry said, "Wait until we inform the general about this. Things just might get a little messy at this Chinese salad bar."

That night, Harry brought General Murphy up-to-date on the two men they had seen. He explained that Amos identified one of them as Quan Phaun, a former employer, and was able to describe the other man. General Murphy told them that Peter Masters was a member of the FBI and that he was returning to pick up John Adams the next morning. He asked if the Chinese men possibly recognize any of them. Harry told him that they were disguised and that he did not think so. Murphy told him that they should stay away from the restaurant for a couple days.

The moon was shining brightly so George and Laura decided to go for a walk on the beach. Laura commented that much of the beach was black. George explained that some of the rock was actually lava that had helped form the island centuries before. Laura asked, "George, do you ever get scared? I know that I should trust God more, but it seems to me that so many things are going against us and that's a bit scary."

"Laura, fear is a normal reaction to our circumstances, but our trust in God will ultimately overcome those fears if we just keep the faith," George replied. "Honey, I'm sorry I got you into this mess. I feel responsible for you being in danger. Let's stop right here and pray about this matter." They both knelt in the sands of the Hawaiian shore and poured out their fears and concerns to their Father in heaven. It wasn't long before they both felt that the God of the universe had heard their prayers. They rose to their feet with faith reinvigorated and with an expectation that God would work things out for his glory in their lives.

George remarked, "Wow, that was the pause that refreshed." Both of them continued their walk down the beach far happier and more peaceful than they were when they left the cabin.

The next morning, Farrago offered to take George and Laura to one of the other islands where they may not be recognized as easily. They only had about a week left so they agreed to go while Amos and Harry took care of things here. Amos created a new set of licenses for them under their new identity. The names matched their new disguises. He said that he would arrange for them to stay on the beach at the Big Island. He left for a short while and returned in a yacht-sized boat. He showed George how to operate the boat and gave him directions on how to get there and where to dock.

He instructed them, "Meet Harry and me back here in about six days. I'll give you updates by radio, but in the meantime, I'll get your tickets transferred to your new identities as Jack and Jill Lane. The boat radio call sign is Dauphin Shaka, and mine will be Land Rover. Here are a couple of throw-away cell phones you can use to get in touch with General Murphy. Now you guys go and enjoy this part of your honeymoon. Harry and I will help you transfer your bags and gear."

They all pitched in and it wasn't long until George was piloting the yacht across the waters to the Big Island.

The weather was nice the next couple days so the newlyweds lay around, or swam, or whatever they chose. They mostly just enjoyed each other. The third day was different. They got a radio call from Amos. He informed them that there had been a raid on the Chinese restaurant and about twenty individuals on the island had been arrested as enemy espionage agents. This was one of the biggest events since the Pearl Harbor was attacked by the Japanese. The Lees gave thanks for God's work in this matter. They rested better after that.

They used one of the cell phones to contact General Murphy. Murphy was glad to hear from them and was happy to inform them that the Chinese terrorist organization that had headquartered in the restaurant had been shut down and that Amos and Harry were interrogating the prisoners one by one.

"The information they are gleaning from these agents is of tremendous value, and it's all because you guys went out for pizza," George said. "I believe that God sent us there, General."

Murphy agreed as they continued to chat for a couple minutes, then he said, "Call me tomorrow about this," and hung up.

George and Laura were anchored in a small bay so they decided to take a swim because of the privacy. They quietly swam while staying near both the shore and the boat.

George swam over to Laura and she said, "I am so happy, even happier that I was back at the hotel. It's been the best honeymoon I've ever had," Laura said with a hearty laugh. "Of all my seventeen marriages, this is the best."

George smiled as he wiped his forehead. "You had me worried there for a second until you mentioned the number 17."

Laura kissed George as they paddled about. "Oh, I miscounted, it was just…"

George smothered the number with a lingering kiss.

After the kiss broke, he said, "Follow me and I'll make you forget all the other marriages."

Laura giggled as she followed George to the boat. They had a nice nap and were eating a snack when the radio sounded, "Dauphin Shaka, this is Land Rover, over."

George got up, keyed the transmit button, and answered, "Land Rover, this is Dauphin Shaka, go ahead."

"Dauphin Shaka, have you heard about the nest being broken up?" Amos asked.

George answered, "Yes, Big Cheese informed us a bit earlier, Land Rover."

"HC and I have been examining the eggs, and we have learned some critical information about the bird population, so we probably ought to meet and discuss what we have learned," Amos advised. "Over."

George answered, "Roger on that, Land Rover, how about the inn in two hours?

"Roger will-co, Dauphin Shaka out," Amos said, ending the radio contact.

George and Laura finished their snacks then headed toward Amos's cabin. The water remained fairly calm on the way over. Amos and Harry were waiting at the small wharf and walked over to the boat as George docked. They told George that they had one of the leaders in the cabin. George was anxious to meet him and hear about their plans.

They entered the room where Amos and Harry had been interrogating the prisoner. Shu Mein grimaced as the heard his interrogators enter.

George asked, "Mr. Mein, we've never met, but I hope to get to know you quite well before I leave. Now I would like to know what your plans are for the future of your organization. Would you be so kind as to enlighten me about that?"

Shu Mein inhaled deeply and said, "I really don't know anything about our leader's future plans, sir."

George said, "Why, Mr. Shu Mein, I thought you would have learned by now that it doesn't pay to prevaricate."

"Please do not start that over again, I don't think I can last much longer if you continue," Shu Mein said.

George yelled into Shu's ear, "Oh really, do you want to reconsider your answer then, Mr. Mein? I'm going to have my assistant grab his things off the table and allow you an opportunity to tell the truth, but if you continue lying, he will be happy to hone his skills a bit more."

Mein began shaking. "Sir, they will kill my family if they find out I have said anything."

George softened his voice, "I understand your concern. I felt the same thing when your people threatened my family. I'm not quite sure, but if you cooperate, I just might be able to get your family out of danger and give you and them a safe haven and a change of identity to each of you, and you can live happily ever after in some quiet village on the mainland. What do you say to that? If not, my assistant is ready, sir."

"That would make me a traitor, and I'm not sure I can live with myself if I reveal information," Shu Mein answered.

"Mr. Mein, time is wasting, but I'll give you one more chance. Before I do, my assistant will remind you of the pain associated with resistance," George said as Harry thrust the acupuncture needles into Mein's shoulders. Mein screamed with pain and his eyes rolled back in his head. Amos poured ice water on Mein's head, and he gasped as he became conscious.

"We can't let you escape the object of this session by passing out, Mr. Mein. Now what do you say about a deal. One more chance for your family, and that's it."

Mein thought a second and then shook his head yes and slumped down with a look of shame as he began relating what he knew about the cartel's plans for future targets. After he told several details, he asked about the deal.

Harry answered, "Give us the names and locations of your family, and we will try to rescue them. Also give us something that will prove to them that you have agreed to this action. If these things you have told us check out, we'll do our best to get your family out."

Amos took George into the room where the scrambler phone was located and he called General Murphy and reported the details Mein had given him.

General Murphy was elated. "I'll have this verified and see what unfolds as the result. Good work, George. Harry and Amos got quite a bit of information from some of the other prisoners. I can't believe how much your honeymoon has aided in the fight against terrorism and halting the enemy's aggression."

George told him about his promise to get his family out of harm's way if possible. General Murphy told him that he would see what he could do.

"If what you have told me proves to be true, then getting his family out and giving Mein a safe haven will be worth it."

George and Amos returned to where Mein waited. "Mr. Mein, I believe that you will be with your family in a short time if the things you have told us pan out."

Shu Mein smiled and said, "Thank you, Major Lee. I thought you could get it done."

"You knew who I was all this time," George exclaimed. "How did you know that?"

Mein answered, "I studied your picture, listened to recordings of your voice from the White House tapes. We have been keeping tabs on you ever since you got that assignment. We lost you here in Hawaii after someone broke into your room. You are considered a high priority target in our community."

About that time, an alarm went off, and after Amos checked the monitors, he indicated that Harry should get Laura inside. A helicopter was heard coming around the mountain.

He shouted, "Get her inside! Now!" He grabbed the prisoner and pushed him toward the room with the sliding door. Harry joined them with Laura in tow as they ran through the door and headed to the eye and hand print recognition door. As the door slid open, they heard alarms being activated. The rock door slid closed behind them.

Once inside, Amos slammed Mein to the floor and checked him over for a signaling device.

"I can't believe I missed that before."

Mein said, "I activated it when you started torturing me."

"So all the things you told us were false," Amos said as he slammed his fist into Mein's face. Mein was out like a light. He lay there as Amos roped him to the door and flipped a switch that would trigger explosives if the enemy entered the room. They heard explosions in the tunnel as Mein's men entered it. Amos grabbed a few things that he might need as he directed the group toward a back door. The door opened to an elevator. They entered and Amos pressed a button. The elevator moved quite rapidly in diagonally upward direction through the mountain. As the elevator door closed behind them at the top, an explosion from below sealed the shaft.

"The agents will be unable to know what was behind the door," Amos said with a pleased look.

"What about all your stuff and that boat?" Harry asked.

"Oh, don't worry about that, it was paid for by those enemy agents anyway," he said with a laugh. "I'll be back in a bit." He entered a side room and was gone at least ten minutes. When he returned, he was dressed like a politician with handlebar mustache. He now sported an English accent.

"Hello, I am Haywood Edwards. Would anyone care for a spot of tea?" They all had a good laugh at Amos's transformation. Suddenly, the mountain quaked and the faint sound of a massive explosion reached them from around the mountain.

Laura asked, "Was that what I think it was?"

George said, "I wouldn't have wanted to be trying to get into that room. Also, I'm reasonably sure that Mr. Mein has no more worries about anything except things of eternity."

Amos said, "I'm sure we will all be safe here tonight. More than likely everyone who landed in that helicopter are no longer around to tell anyone about what they found because the whole area was rigged with C-4. The only possible surviving person would have been on the boat, and that was only if he had a gas mask on, because it was rigged to set off poisonous gas. That trigger was activated with the same switch that started the timer for the explosives. You will find clothes that should fit in your rooms which I've had prepared for some time now."

The news that evening reported that the volcano had made some rumblings, but there was nothing about an explosion. Amos drove Harry some distance away before he was allowed to use the burner phone and reported to

General Murphy about events of the afternoon. Murphy was glad that everyone had gotten out safely.

"The CIA is investigating the scene of the explosions, but have come up with nothing but a burnt-out helicopter and lots of dead bodies. We found that much of what Mr. Mein told you was true, but his family didn't check out. He must have thought you would know if he was lying so he gave you correct information about their plans. He probably believing you would be captured or killed by his agents."

Harry asked, "What about the boat at the dock?"

Murphy answered, "There was a boat found, but it was registered to a Mr. Haywood Edwards. He will pick it up at his convenience according to his butler."

"Do you mean to tell me that Mr. Edwards has a butler?" Harry asked. "Wait till I tell Laura and George. General, Mr. Edwards is actually Amos Farrago."

General Murphy laughed so hard that he could hardly tell Harry to call him the next day.

After the call, Harry deleted the phone number and wiped the outside clean of his fingerprints. He pulled the battery and the SIM card and tossed it into the ocean on the way back to the cabin area. Amos gave Harry directions back to the mansion as he left to pick up the yacht.

Harry had been back at the mansion and was talking with George out on the veranda only for a short while when they saw the lift coming up the side of the mountain. It stopped at veranda and Amos got off. Harry walked over to meet him and said, "Man, you've thought of everything, haven't you?"

Amos answered, "I've tried, but we all make mistakes, just like back at the cabin. That's why you plan to deal with the mistakes as they occur."

They all slept well that evening and awoke refreshed, except for Laura who had worried most of the night over those who had died during their raid on Amos's cabin. The cook eased things a bit when he brought them a delicious breakfast. As they ate, George asked Harry about Tommy and Pam.

Harry said, "Pam is good and Tommy is growing like a weed. Before I came here, we moved to the new base. It's a really nice place. I think that you and Laura will like it too."

Laura blurted out, "We probably will if we can get off this Island alive."

Amos spoke up, "Laura, I think that most of the troublemakers are out of the picture, and things will begin to get better. In fact, the yacht was decontaminated so it's safe for you and George to go back over to the quiet beach on the Big Island again today if you'd like."

Laura looked at George with expectation. "Okay, I think we can do that. We will leave soon after breakfast if Amos, ah, Mr. Edwards will show us how to get down the mountainside to the boat."

Amos agreed so George and Laura were able to continue their honeymoon over on the beach at the Big Island.

## HOME SWEET HOME

The rest of the honeymoon went quickly and without incident. The day they were to fly out on the red-eye flight arrived too quickly. George returned the yacht to Amos. It didn't take long for Laura and George to get into their disguises, and Amos instructed his driver to drive them to the Honolulu airport. After they entered the limo, Amos handed Laura and George their tickets and IDs, which read Donald Davis and Donna Davis. George said as he looked at the pictures on the IDs side by side.

"A nice-looking couple don't you think, Donna, honey?"

"I was able to open a bank account in those names and here are a couple credit cards just in case you need some funds before you get your new cards from your bank,"

Amos told them as he presented each of them a card with their AKA names on them.

"Amos," George said, "I could never thank you enough for all that you have done for Laura and me. Except for Harry here, you have been kinder to me than anyone else in the world. May God's richest blessings rest upon you. And thank you for being so gracious as to allow us the use of your mansion and your yacht."

Amos responded, "George, when you trusted me enough to let me go back there on that island after we first met, I felt I owed you my life. You, through that trust and your efforts in getting that weapon completed, have saved my family's lives. It is I who could never repay you for what you have done for me. It was through your influence that led me to find Jesus Christ as my Savior. With your permission and God's grace, I will continue to watch out for you and Laura. Thank you for your trusting me and getting this Harry guy to cooperate with you. You are right, Harry is a good friend to you, and he respects you as much as I do."

George didn't know how to respond so he just reached over and shook Amos's hand and thanked him. About that time, they were pulling up to the terminal. The driver came around and opened the door for the passengers and then went to the trunk and retrieved three bags and handed them to the trio.

"Compliments of Mr. Edwards."

Amos said, "I think I had better leave you three now. You have my number, so when you get settled, use these names and the phones inside the bags to contact me. If for nothing else, call me just to say hello. I'll be seeing you. God bless you both greatly."

Amos and his driver shook each of their hands, got into the limo, and left.

They watched until the limo drove out of the terminal area then headed inside. They checked their baggage as carry on luggage and took seats to await boarding. It took about seven hours to reach California. Once they arrived at the San Francisco International Airport, a driver for General Murphy approached Harry and asked about George and Laura. He said he had a car waiting for them for them, but had not seen them come out of the terminal.

Harry asked to see his ID before he told him, "Lieutenant Lions, this is Major George Lee and his wife Laura."

The lieutenant looked perplexed. "But they look nothing like they look in the pictures I was given."

George shook the officer's hand and said, "Do they look anything like these?"

"Yes, but the names are different, "Lt. Lions said.

Harry told him that the situation required disguises and new identities for George and Laura, so the officer led them out of the terminal without further questioning. After they got into the staff car, he asked, "Are you good folk okay? General Murphy said that there had been some trouble over there, but he didn't get specific."

"Yes, we are okay!" George answered. "We had a lot of help from General Murphy and some good folk like Lt. Harry Collins here."

Lt. Lions said, "General Murphy told me about you folk and how important you were in the success of his last assignment. It's an honor to finally meet all three of you. I am to put you in a motel until I get orders about which set of parents you are to visit," Lt. Lions said, then asked, "Where would you like to go first?"

George said, "Honey, I think we aught to see your parents first, is that all right with you?"

Laura said it would be okay so the lieutenant said he would make the arrangements for that flight. He asked, "Lt. Collins, I guess you will be headed back to the base, won't you?"

Harry nodded that he would.

"All right then, I'll make the arrangements for you to get back as well," Lt. Lions told Harry.

Turning toward the Lees, he asked "Now you two, which names are you flying under, the Lees or Davis?"

Laura answered, "I think it will be better if we keep Davis for now because we are already disguised as them if that's okay."

Lt. Lions agreed, "I think that will be fine, so I will make the arrangements, then report what's happened to General Murphy. Do you have a phone number so he can contact with you?"

George opened his bag and found a phone and gave the number to the lieutenant. He thanked him and headed back into the terminal to schedule the flights. He returned in a bit, handed the three of them their tickets, and said, "We can forget about the motel because you guys will be flying out on the same flight to St. Louis where the Lt. Collins will transfer flights. You and Mrs. Lee will continue on to Maine to see your parents."

George said, "Sounds good to me. How much time do we have before the flight leaves?"

"About forty-five minutes," the lieutenant answered. At that, they all got out and headed back into the terminal. Lt. Lions stopped just outside the door and said, "Major and Mrs. Lee, I wish you the best and I'm sorry your honeymoon was interrupted so many ways. God bless you both in the future." He saluted, then shook hands with Harry. "Lt. Collins, it was good to meet you. I guess I will see you back on base in a couple days. I have some business to attend to for General Murphy while I'm here, but I will be back there soon."

Harry and the Lees headed inside the airline terminal. In a short while, the three of them were headed toward their families. Harry called Pam and told George and Laura that she had given them her regards. They said that Harry should do the same for them. After Harry finished the call, George and he talked until the "fasten seat belts" sign came on. George and Laura gave Harry a hug before he exited the plane. Only about ten passengers got off at St. Louis, and only three passengers boarded so they were soon taxiing on to the runway and were airborne toward Laura's home state before they knew it.

They landed safely, and because they had only a couple carry-on bags, they soon were seated in a rental SUV headed northward toward her parents house guided by an in-vehicle GPS. Laura was getting excited about seeing her parents and could hardly keep still. She was so nervous that she chattered like a small child.

George finally asked, "Do you have your nerve tablets with you?"

"What do you mean, George?" she asked, but then understood, "Oh, I'm doing it, aren't I?"

"You were doing pretty well at it too," George laughed. "If the console wasn't dividing us, I'd ask you to come over here and give me a hug, you little cutie pie."

Laura said, "Stop it, you're embarrassing me. I can't help it if I'm excited about going home."

It took about an hour to get to her parent's home. They walked to the front door and rang the bell. Laura's dad answered the door. He said, "Hello, may I help you folk?"

George said, "We are the Lees, and we are looking for a place to spend a few days while we catch up on our rest."

Mr. Krieger said, "I'm sorry, but there is a motel about five blocks down on Main Street. I'm sure they would be happy to rent you a room."

About that time, Shirley Krieger came to the door. "Simon, what's going on, who are these nice people?"

He answered, "They said they were the Lees looking for a place to rest, dear."

"The Lees," Mrs. Krieger said thoughtfully. "Are you related to George Lee?"

Finally, Laura could take it no longer and yelled happily, "Dad, Mom, it's George and Laura."

They both looked shocked, but Mom recognized Laura's voice and ran out the door and grabbed her in a big bear hug and cried as though she had not seen here in years.

"Oh, honey, I've been so concerned about you, knowing you were in Hawaii when that volcano erupted."

Laura said, "That was not a volcano rumbling, but I'll tell you more about it later."

Dad asked, "What are you two doing in that getup? It isn't Halloween."

George said, "We'll explain more about that later too, if that's okay."

"Of course, come right on in here," Simon said. "You don't have to go to Main Street, you have a place to rest right here for as long as you need it."

George picked their bags up and they went inside. They visited for a while, then Mrs. Krieger asked if they would like some dinner.

George said, "Sounds good. How about Laura and I take you two out to eat?"

"Are you sure?" Simon Krieger asked.

Then Shirley noticed that Laura didn't have a purse. "Laura, what happened to your purse, was it stolen?"

She answered, "No, not really, let's just say it was involved in that volcanic eruption you heard about."

"Really," Shirley exclaimed, "how in the world did that happen?"

Laura explained a bit of what happened as they walked to the rental. Simon sat up front with George and Laura and her mom sat in the back. Simon gave directions to the restaurant. They entered and several people said hello to the Kriegers and looked at their friends with inquiring eyes.

The waiter led them to a table in the center of the restaurant, but George asked to be seated at a table in the corner. Laura understood the caution after the dangers they had faced over the last few days. He had the vantage point of seeing all the entrances to the dining room and felt secure that no one could sneak up behind him. The waiter returned with their drink orders and a note he handed to George.

He looked at it and asked, "Where did this come from?"

The waiter looked over toward a table where a man sat waving at them. Laura and George recognized Amos immediately. George excused himself from the table and walked over to Amos.

"Won't you join us Amos?"

"I think its best that you visit with your in-laws," Amos responded, "but it's good to see that you made it safely. Actually, I was on the flights all the way with you. I had a great disguise, I guess. I saw you messing with your in-laws at their front door. Hey, enjoy your meal. I'll be in contact, George."

George shook Amos's hand and walked back over to the family's table. Laura had a look of unbelief on her face so George told her he would explain later.

"Do you know someone living here?" Shirley asked.

Laura said, "It's a friend that happened to be in town at the same time."

They were having a great evening until Simon said, "I've got to be at work early in the morning, so we had better get back home so I can get my beauty rest."

Surprisingly, things went well during the whole week spent with the Kriegers. George and Laura were both relieved. They took comfort in the fact that Amos had made contact with them.

It soon became time for them to catch a flight to George's parents. Laura dreaded to leave, but accepted it as part of life now that she had done it several times. Her mother cried as they boarded the plane. As they were walking to their seats, George glanced around the plane, and sure enough, Amos was seated a couple aisles over and three seats behind them. He gave Amos a hello with his eyes. Amos's eyes gave George the sign to look back.

Entering the plane were a couple of oriental-looking men. George sat down in his assigned seat, but watched the men seat themselves behind Amos. Amos gave him a sign that indicated he knew who the men were.

George whispered an alert to Laura, "Honey, did you see those oriental-looking men who just boarded?"

She acknowledged that she had, "Do you know them?"

"No," George responded, "but I think they are after Amos. We need to keep an eye on them."

Laura agreed, and so during the flight to Atlanta, she kept a close eye on them. She noted that when George moved around, they paid no attention, but when Amos moved around, one of them always stuck close by him.

When they were transferring planes, Amos went into the bathroom and one of the men followed him inside. George and Laura kept an eye on the other man. When the man or Amos came back out after a considerable time, the second man went into the restroom. This time, George followed him. He walked over to one of the lavatories and began washing his hands. Out of the corner of his eye, he watched the man search for Amos and his partner. Several people came in and used the facility and left. It appeared that Amos and the man's partner were not here. The man looked confused and started for the door. Suddenly, a stall door opened and Amos leaped. The man's reflexes were cat-like. He grabbed Amos and flung him on to one of the lavatories where he writhed in pain. George sprung toward the man and judo chopped him across the neck. He slumped to floor, but came back up swinging. George dodged the lightning-fast punches and laid an uppercut on the chin of the surprised man. Amos had recovered and jumped on the man's back and had him in a sleeper hold. George was able to get in another couple punches. Amos pulled the unconscious man into a stall and locked the door. George called General Murphy and told him where the two suspected enemy agents could be located. They watched for about fifteen minutes until four well-dressed men in black suits arrived looking in the area where George had told Murphy the men would be. They found them leaning over commodes with hands tied around the pipes with their own shoestrings.

Outside the restroom, Amos and George told Laura what had happened and laughed at the surprised look on the second agent's face when George avoided his swing.

Amos said, "Laura, he's almost as good as you."

They were laughing together as the men were dragged out of the restroom in handcuffs by the CIA agents.

Amos looked at George. "I owe you again. You probably saved my neck that last guy probably would have probably taken me out, but with your help, you kept me from being captured or worse. Thanks, Major Lee. My respect for you becomes deeper the longer I am acquainted with you."

Laura said, "I knew I had one of the good ones, but listening to you, I'm beginning to think I have the best."

"Come on you two," George said. "You are embarrassing me. Don't you think we had better get ready to board our flight?"

Laura said, "I think we have about an hour to wait so let's get something to eat."

They agreed, but after seeing the prices of food in the terminal, they changed their minds and headed back to wait for their call to board the flight. It took a while to board after the boarding call came. They sat some rows apart from Amos, just in case.

This flight was uneventful except for a little turbulence near the Missouri River area just before the descent into the Sioux City, Iowa Airport. They invited Amos to come to the farm and stay with George's parents. He agreed on condition that it would be no problem to the parents.

They drove a rental vehicle to the farm as Amos looked at all the corn fields and said, "It reminds me of the *Field of Dreams* movie."

George said, "Actually, that isn't too far from our farm. If you like big fields, you will like the Lee ranch."

They arrived at the farm just before suppertime. They knocked on the door, and Paul Lee came and opened it. He looked at the three people standing at the door, and quick as a flash, he reached inside the door and brought a shotgun around to his waist and said, "Identify yourselves or I will blow you to kingdom come."

George yelled, "Dad, it's us, George and Laura and one of our friends."

Paul Lee lowered the shotgun and said, "The voice sounds like George's, but you don't look a thing like him."

George said, "We had to put on these disguises so we could get away from some bad guys, Dad."

Paul yelled, "Sally, come here, we got a guy out here that claims to be our son, George."

Charlene and Sally Lee came running.

Sally asked, "Paul, you're right. Which one says he's George?"

George spoke up, "Mom, it's me, George. And this is Laura. Don't you remember how that we were supposed to visit after our honeymoon?"

Laura said, "Mrs. Lee, it really is us. We'll tell you why we are made up like this if you will let us come in."

"Who's that feller there with you guys?" Paul asked.

George said, "This is a friend of ours, Amos Farrago. He's been a lot of help over the last few days, Dad."

Sally said, "Paul, it sounds like them, so have them come in. Do you guys have any ID?"

"Mom, did you hear about the volcano acting up over in Hawaii? Well, when that happened, all our stuff was destroyed. That's why we had to put this get up on so we could escape Hawaii and get back to see you guys. We will show you what we have, but we lost everything in an explosion. Please believe us!"

Amos spoke up, "Mr. and Mrs. Lee, if you will allow George to go into the bathroom, he can get out of his disguise and show you that he actually is George, your son."

"Sounds good to me," Paul said. "Charlene, get the pistol from the kitchen drawer and follow him to the bathroom and watch him close. If he makes any false move, put a slug in him."

It took a few minutes, but when George returned, Charlene was following him with a big grin on her face.

Sally said, "Son, it really is you. Paul, put down that gun and get over here and give your son a hug."

Paul's face brightened as he looked at George and placed the shotgun back near the front door. He hurried over and gave George and Laura hugs. "Now who did you say this guy was?"

George said, "Dad, this is Amos Farrago, he has saved Laura's and my lives more than once."

Paul reached out and shook hands. "It's great to meet one of George's friends, Mr. Farrago."

Amos said, "George has saved my life more than once as well. You have a great son, Mr. Lee."

George grabbed Charlene and gave her a hug. "How are you and Lt. Klink getting along?"

Charlene answered, "We had a few dates, but things didn't seem to click with us after a while. We are still friends though."

Laura suggested, "Perhaps you and Amos will hit it off. He'd be a pretty nice catch."

"They would be good for each other, don't you think?" she asked as George shook his head in agreement.

"Quit trying to be my big brother," Charlene protested. "I can pick out my own boyfriends, thank you very much."

Amos added, "Yes, quit trying to be my big brother too. I can pick out my own girlfriends, too."

"Okay, you guys," George said. "You're already working together. It's already begun."

Charlene and Amos laughed, and Amos said, "Do you want to go get a coke, Charlene?"

She said, "Sure, I'll drive."

They walked out to Charlene's Cadillac and she yelled back, "Mom. Dad, we'll be back in a few minutes."

George opened the back door and looked around. There were CIA agents watching him from several locations. He learned that there was an agent positioned across the road watching the front of the house. He identified himself, "George and Laura Lee here."

One of the agents came out of the shadows and approached George. They shook hands as he said, "Hello, I'm Agent Brown. General Murphy informed us that you and your wife were coming, but he didn't mention the other guy was coming."

"He is a good friend of ours whom we invited along," George replied, "and my sister and he went out for a Coke."

The agent asked, "We know. Our man at the front informed. What's his name?"

George answered, "We call him Amos. I'll introduce him when he get's back."

Agent Brown agreed, "I'll be looking forward to meeting him. Any friend of Major Lee's must be a special man or woman. We'll see you in a little while."

George waved as Agent Brown left him.

When he got inside, he phoned Amos, and after Amos answered, he asked, "Hey, Amos, what alias did you come here under?"

"Let me think, I think it's the Edwards from Hawaii," Amos answered. "Why?"

"Well," George said, "I just talked to a CIA Agent named Brown, and he asked your name. I told him we called you Amos."

Amos hesitated, "Okay, how about me acting like it is because I like Amos and Andy, the old radio program."

"That will be great, Amos," George agreed. "I told him I'd introduce you when you came back."

About that time, Laura and his mom came looking for him.

"There you are, we thought you had run off like Amos," Laura said.

"No, I have two beautiful ladies and a handsome fellow to keep me busy here," George suggested.

"Why, honey, you are so sweet to say things like that," Sally said with a smile as she walked over to give George a hug. "It's so good to have Laura and you here for a few days. That is, of course, unless another helicopter doesn't come and pick you up like it did the last time you visited."

George answered, "I don't expect that to happen. Maybe we can have a week that is peaceful and safe, especially the way Pop acted so quickly when he didn't recognize the three of us."

George, Laura, Mom, and Dad Lee were having a good visit when Charlene and Amos returned. They entered all excited and talking as though they were old friends.

Charlene was chattering excitedly, "Dad and Mom, you ought to have heard some of the stuff that Amos told about George and Laura."

George got excited then. "Amos, you haven't told her anything about the place out in the ocean? Have you?"

"No, George, I was just telling her how you saved my life back in Atlanta and how we waited until the CIA came and hauled those two guys away," Amos said.

"Come on, Amos," George looked upset. "You shouldn't even be telling her things like that. Mom and Dad will be worried sick now."

Dad Lee spoke up, "No, son, I have an idea that you have done some pretty dangerous stuff, or we wouldn't have CIA guarding our home like they do. I can't even go milk

Bossy without stepping on one of those guys. I know they mean well, but it's hard to farm with them under foot."

"Amos, that reminds me, I have to introduce you to Agent Brown," George said. "What are we going to tell him about the difference between your ID and the name I gave him?"

"I got it covered, George," Amos replied. "Let's go get this over with, so we can get back in here and visit." He led the way to the back door as Mom Lee pulled some fresh baked cookies out of the oven.

She called as they opened the door, "Hey, George, ask if those agents would like some warm cookies and milk or coffee."

Amos whispered, "Is she for real, George? It's no wonder you think and act the way you do if she treated everybody like this when you were growing up."

"Yes," George answered, "she's for real. Hey, Agent Brown, come and meet Amos."

Agent Brown approached them. "How are you doing? I'm Agent Sammy Brown, Amos. Could I see some ID, please?"

As they shook hands, Amos reached into his pocket and pulled out his wallet and removed a picture ID. "Here you go, Agent Brown. I'm Amos Edwards."

Agent Brown looked at the picture then at Amos and smiled. "Looks great, and that takes care of my inquisitive nature. Thank you very much."

"Hey," George said, "my mom said that we should ask you guys if you wanted some fresh baked cookies and milk or coffee."

Agent Brown whistled and yelled loudly, "Cookies!"

Agents appeared out of nowhere. Agent Brown told George, "She has done this every night since we've been here. If she keeps this up, we all will have to go on some sort of exercise program and go on a special diet. But they are the best cookies I've ever tasted anywhere."

They headed back inside as the agents formed a line. Mom Lee had the cookies in sandwich bags and the agents were passing them back to the end of the line until each member had a bag of cookies.

She yelled, "How many want coffee?"

There were three hands raised.

"Now, how many want milk?"

Four raised their hands. She passed the orders down the line like she had done the cookies, then they all left, disappearing into the night.

Inside, George and Amos joined the others sitting at the kitchen table. There was also chili soup and cornbread in addition to the milk and cookies. Everyone was eating by the time George and Amos were seated. To Amos, it was exciting. It was like something from an old movie, but he loved it.

He asked Charlene, "Can you cook like your mom?"

Charlene looked surprised. "Why do you ask?"

"Well, if you can, I was going to ask you to marry me," Amos answered. "My cook can't cook this good. Mom Lee, these are delicious fixings."

Charlene smiled. "Hey, you guys. Did you hear that? I think that Amos just proposed to Charlene. Did you hear that, Laura?"

"Yes, I'm pretty sure I did, Charlene," Laura said. "Dad Lee, you had better go get your shotgun while Mom Lee goes and calls the preacher."

Everyone about rolled from the laughter, except Amos.

He looked at Charlene with a serious look, "Charlene, I really wasn't kidding. I don't care if you can cook or not, will you marry me?"

Charlene turned red faced. "You're serious?"

"Yes! I am definitely serious," Amos asked. "Will you marry me, Charlene?"

"But we haven't had our first kiss," Charlene stuttered, "and you and I don't know each other very well."

Amos said, "I can fix that." He got up from the table and went over to Charlene's chair, pulled it out, swung it around and gave her a big kiss. "We will take the next few days to get to know each other."

Charlene looked around and tears streamed down her cheeks.

Amos look surprised. "Charlene, I'm so sorry if I hurt you."

She got up and ran from to the room.

He looked around. "I'm sorry, but I thought she just might feel the same way I do. Please excuse me." He got up, took a cookie, and went out to the porch.

Laura followed Charlene and George followed Amos.

When George got out on the porch, Amos said, "George, I'm sorry I messed up the evening for everybody. Please take me to the airport tonight and I'll head back to Hawaii."

George said, "No, Amos. Please just stay and do like you promised and get to know Charlene better."

Amos was adamant. "No, I'm too embarrassed to let anyone see my face, so just go get my bag, and come on and get me to the airport. Please, George."

George went inside and found Amos's bag. He told Mom and Dad he was going to take Amos to the airport. As he was leaving, Laura came down the stairs and asked what was happening.

George told Laura, "Amos asked me to take him to the airport, so I'll be back as soon as I can. Do you want to come with me?"

Laura answered, "Sure, George, let me go get my purse, and I'll be right down."

As Laura was getting her purse, Charlene opened her door and entered the hallway.

"What's going on, Laura?"

Laura said, "George and I are driving Amos to the airport. He's leaving because he embarrassed you and embarrassed himself in front of everyone this evening."

Charlene looked surprised. "No. Amos shouldn't leave because of that."

Laura went down the stairs and went out to the rental where George and Amos were waiting for her. Charlene watched from her upstairs window as they drove away. She suddenly broke into tears and ran down the stairs, but it was too late to catch them. She told Mom and Dad Lee that she would be back in a little while and went running out to her car. She fumbled for her keys and was so nervous that after she found them, she had trouble getting them into the ignition. Finally, she sped away after the vehicle that was taking away the only man she had finally decided she had ever truly loved. She prayed, "God, please help me catch that vehicle before they get to the airport."

It was a good thing that the state troopers were patrolling somewhere else because she would have gotten a speeding ticket had they been on the road at that time. Tires squealed on the curves. It took about twenty minutes to catch the SUV, and when she did, she pulled over into the passing lane and came up even with George's vehicle, honked her horn, and motioned for him to pull over. Over Amos's protests, George pulled the vehicle over and stopped. Charlene pulled to a stop in back of it and ran up to the window where Amos was setting. At first he refused to look at her. Finally, she talked him into getting into the car with her.

"Ride with me a bit, and if you still want to go to the airport, I'll take you there myself." She yelled at George, "You two go on back to the house. Amos and I have some talking to do."

George handed Amos his bags and got back into the rental and left them sitting in her car.

It took several minutes for Laura and George to get back to the house where Mom and Dad were still waiting at the kitchen table.

Mom asked, "We figured that you two would be back in a short while, the way Charlene shot out of here. What happened?"

Laura replied, "Charlene chased us down and we pulled over. Charlene talked Amos into getting into the car with her. She told him that after they talked a bit, if he still wanted to leave, she would drive him to the airport herself."

Paul Lee laughed. "That girl beats all I ever seen. I think she fell for the guy before they left for their little jaunt to get a Coke."

George walked around the table and sat down beside Dad, and Laura took a seat beside Sally Lee.

George said, "Finally, the Lees sitting around the table as a family. I thought this would be a quiet visit, but I don't think I can take much more of this kind of quietness, if this is what it's like. Hey, you guys, tell us about how you are getting along over a cup of coffee and some cookies."

They were laughing and talking when Amos and Charlene walked in the front, laughing and talking like nothing had ever happened.

George said, "It didn't take you very long for you to work things out. What happened?"

Charlene smiled. "Tomorrow, Amos and I are going into town to look for a ring. What do you say to that, Mom? Dad, Amos has something to ask you."

"What do you want to ask me, son?" Dad Lee asked.

"Mr. Lee," Amos began, "I didn't use the right approach before, and so I'll try again. Mr. Lee, may I have your permission to marry your daughter?"

Mr. Lee thought for a second. "Will you be able to take care of my daughter as well or better than she's taken care of now?

"I'm not quite sure how well taken care of she is now, but I can assure you, sir, that I can afford her every benefit possible," Amos replied.

Mr. Lee looked at George and asked, "Son, is he really able to do that?"

George answered, "I believe from what I've seen that he can."

Yes," Laura said with a nod of agreement.

"Mom, what do you say?" Mr. Lee asked.

Mrs. Lee said, "Oh, stop stalling, can't you see that Charlene is prancing. Just tell him yes."

"Well, I guess that settles it then, Mr. Amos, you are welcome to my daughter's hand in marriage if she is willing to marry you," Mr. Lee responded.

"Oh, thank you, Mr. Lee," Amos said. "I usually just take something if I want it badly enough, but Charlene said she wouldn't marry me if I didn't ask you, so thank you for agreeing, sir."

"Son, you had better get used to listening to her," Mr. Lee said as he chuckled. "It's just the beginning."

Charlene walked over to her dad and gave him a hug and a kiss on the cheek, then turned and gave Amos a lingering kiss. "I know it was hard, but I promise I'll make it up to you. Thanks for doing that for me, Mr. Edwards."

They all congratulated Amos and Charlene. After that, Dad Lee said, "I'm headed for the bed there's been way too much excitement for one evening. I'm saying good night to you all."

"Good night, Dad," George said.

Then Mom decided to follow him and said, "Amos has anyone shown you to your room?"

"Actually, no," Amos answered, "everything has just been so hectic and I was too distracted. Besides that, I decided to leave before anyone had a chance to show it to me."

Charlene said, "I'm going to bed pretty soon, I'll show him where it is when I go up."

George and Laura left Amos and Charlene munching cookies and drinking coffee at the kitchen table and headed upstairs. They were so tired that after they entered the quiet of their room, it did not take either of them long before they both were sleeping soundly.

The next morning, they went downstairs and there sat Charlene and Amos sound asleep leaning over the table.

Mom Lee was fixing breakfast and told them, "It's good to see you guys up and about. I let you guys sleep in because I figured you were wore out from the big fracas you had last night. Dad is probably about done out in the barn. He's usually done by about seven o'clock. I let Charlene and Amos sleep in too, bless their hearts, all this romance stuff is hard on a person, you know?"

Laura said to Mom Lee, "You are so sweet for letting all of us sleep in. George is supposed to show me around today and maybe take us horseback riding. That is, if you don't have anything for me to do here."

Mom Lee said, "I got something for you to do, but it can wait until after you get done outside. Dad and I still ride some. Maybe we all could go riding together."

Charlene raised her head. "Mom, do I smell biscuits?" She looked at her watch and jumped to her feet. "My lands, I'm late for work." She reached for her cell phone as she hurried upstairs to get the things needed for work. They heard her talking with her boss as her voice grew muffled as she entered her room.

Amos was awake now, a bit disheveled, he looked around. "Oh, hello everybody. I'm losing my touch being around you folks. Normally, I would have never slept with someone making noise near me. Oh well, what smells so good? I guess Charlene and I didn't make it to bed. Where is she?"

Laura answered, "Charlene is late for work Amos. She went upstairs to get things she needs for work."

About that time, they heard Dad Lee enter the back door whistling "God Is So Great."

"Well, it sure sounds like somebody is in a good mood today," George said.

"Yes sir-re-bob," Dad Lee cheerfully answered. "Mom, those CIA guys said that those donuts were delicious, and if you keep making such good coffee, Starbacks just might be put out of business."

"Bless their hearts. They work hard keeping us safe. I feel that feeding them is the least I can do for them," Mom Lee said.

Charlene came running down the stairs and into the kitchen and said, "Good-bye, everyone. Sorry, I have something important to do today at work. Amos, would you like to walk me to my car?" They walked out the front door together, chatting.

The rest of the group were almost finished eating when Amos came back in. Mom Lee jumped up and got him a cup of coffee.

"You look like you could really use this, Amos."

He replied, "I sure can. Thanks, Mrs. Lee." Turning toward George, he asked, "Will it be okay if I borrow the car to go meet Charlene during lunch?"

"Sure, Laura and I, and maybe Mom and Dad are going horseback riding today after breakfast anyway," George answered.

Amos sat down and began devouring his eggs, bacon, and toast, and of course, a couple donuts.

Dad Lee looked up at George and said, "Hey, horseback riding sounds great. George, have you forgotten how to saddle a horse?"

George answered, "I don't think so, but you can watch me just in case I make a mistake. Let's go and get them ready." As they left, he told Laura, "This should only take a few minutes so maybe Mom has something you could wear while you are riding."

Mom said, "Come with me, Laura."

Laura followed her up the stairs and into a clothes closet. She pulled out two outfits: one for her and one for Laura. Laura went into her room and changed while Mom changed in her room.

The two looked like family as they arrived at the corral. The CIA guys were certainly interested in what was going on. Agent Brown came over to where they were mounting.

"Have you got extras for another agent and me?"

George looked over at Dad for approval, and after his nod, he answered, "Sure, I'll go get two more horses. You are welcome to ride along."

Agent Brown yelled, "Clyde, come go with us."

The agent came running. He was out of breath when he got there. "Major Lee, it's an honor to finally meet you. I've heard so much about you from your mom and dad, in addition to General Murphy's occasional updates on you."

George reached out and shook his hand. "Thanks for watching out for my parents."

After the agents helped with saddling the horses, they all mounted and headed out to an open field where the agents moved to each side of the group. They rode for about forty-five minutes when suddenly a shot rang out.

A bullet whizzed by George's head, and he yelled, "Get low and let's get out of here."

He spun his horse around and spurred it into a gallop trying to watch out for his parents and Laura. They approached a shallow depression just low enough to afford them some concealment. They brought the horses to a halt down in it. George dismounted and ran, then low crawled to where he could see from a concealed position.

"Agent Brown, do you have an extra weapon?"

Dad spoke up, "Son, I have a rifle," as he pulled it from the saddle holster on the horse and handed it up to George.

George told his family to stay down and then crawled up to where the agents were lying in the prone position. "Can you see anyone, Agent Brown?"

"I thought I saw someone over in that clump of trees. Here use my binoculars and take a look for yourself," Agent Brown said as he handed them to George and reached for his radio to contact the other agents about their circumstances.

George probed the bushes where the agent had indicated and then remembered that Dad's rifle had a powerful scope. He handed the binoculars back to Agent Brown and grabbed the rifle. When he sighted through its scope, he saw movement and fired. He heard a yell, like someone was startled or maybe injured. He asked Agents Brown and Clyde, "Did you hear that?"

Both of them nodded so George kept watching the location. Agent Brown's radio sounded as the backup team reported that they were coming in on the back side of the attacker's position and asked them to make sure they identified their target before firing in that direction.

Agent Brown responded, "Roger on that."

George kept an eye on the area when suddenly, the suspects burst through with agents in close pursuit.

It wasn't long until the agents apprehended the suspects and took them into custody. They brought them in and searched the area for more suspects, just in case.

Of course, pleasure riding was over, so they mounted their steeds and headed for the barn. By the time they got the horses put back in the stables, the suspects had been brought through the barnyard and loaded into a van. The injured man had been taken away, and Dad, Mom, and Laura had gone into the house. George hung around the van where the uninjured man was held. He heard the CIA agents questioning him, but no information was forthcoming.

George called General Murphy and reported the incident.

"Do you mean to tell me that they got a shot at you George?" General Murphy said excitedly.

"I'd really like for Lt. Collins and me to get our hands on him for a few minutes," George said.

"George, I'll have the uninjured man brought here so Harry can have a shot at him after the CIA is finished with him. Is the family okay?"

"Yes," George said, "Just when Laura and I were enjoying our visit here, and that jerk messed it up. Mom and Dad are scared half to death now. Oh! I almost forgot! Amos proposed to Charlene, and she agreed. What do you think of that?"

"Man, how did that happen so fast?" the general asked. "It must run in the family. There must be something strangely irresistible about the Lee family that attracts people and entices people to want to propose and get married ASAP. I'll see that your captive is available for questioning when you get here. We will talk later. Stay safe."

George heard a chuckle as he hung up the phone.

George left the house and went to the van and knocked on side door. He took a look at the captive.

Agent Brown said, "George, you go on in the house, we'll take care of him.

George remarked as he stared at the man in handcuffs, "I just wanted to see what the weasel looked like that took a shot at me from an ambush." Then he addressed the handcuffed man, "I've made sure we meet again."

The man suddenly became very agitated, and with a Vietnamese accent, he said, "Hey, I've heard about you." He turned to the agent and pleaded, "Please don't let him take me. He'll do bad things to me."

George told him, "I feel very sorry for you, but it has already been arranged. Maybe if you cooperate with this man, there will be no need to meet in a few days. Keep our future meeting in mind during your time with the CIA."

Agent Brown grinned. "What a reputation you've built for yourself among our enemies. Good for you. He might talk now that he has met you. Is there anything I can do for you?"

George asked, "Is anyone going into town?"

"Sure, in a couple hours," Agent Brown answered, "we are taking the prisoner into town for transfer to other agents. Would you want a ride?"

"Amos took the rental so he could meet Charlene for lunch. After the incident with the shooter, Laura and I would like to take Mom and Dad to town. We can use Dad's truck, but it would be nice to have some protection."

They finished the conversation after a bit and George headed inside. He found the family sitting at the kitchen table chatting about the shooting and the possibility of future danger. Mom saw George come in.

"There he is, our hero."

"I'm sure glad Dad had that rifle with him," George said.

Dad spoke up, "I determined that if I saw one of those guys that they weren't going to get the chance to hurt your mom and me."

"I think you can be a bit more relaxed now, Dad," George suggested. He looked over at Laura and said, "The CIA agents will be going into town about lunchtime so I thought maybe we all could go in and meet Charlene and Amos for lunch." Then he asked, "Dad and Mom, do you want to go have lunch in town?"

Mom looked over at Dad. "I think I'd like to go with George and Laura. Come on, Dad, and let's go eat with them for a change. I'm so shook up, I don't know if I can cook."

Dad grinned and agreed to go, so Mom Lee and Laura went upstairs to change from their riding clothes into clothing more appropriate for eating in the town's restaurant. While they were upstairs changing, George called Amos to let him know they were headed into town and would like to meet them for lunch. Amos agreed and told them where they were planning to eat.

When the CIA agents learned that everyone was heading into town, Brown appointed them a driver and had an escort van go ahead of the van carrying the family and one following them. As they approached the restaurant, agents exited the lead escort van and went in first. After they assured that it was safe, then the Lees were allowed to go in. Needless to say, the Lees got special service that day. Charlene and Amos arrived before them and watched as the CIA came in and looked things over and then give the okay for the family to enter. They smiled as the Lees entered and came over to their table. Two tables was placed together to make a long one. Mom Lee asked the agents to join them, but this time they refused.

George told Mom, "They act differently when the public is watching, so they can't do that now." It seemed that she was satisfied with that answer so she didn't insist.

Dad remarked, "Is all this attention necessary, George?"

"They just want to make sure nothing happens here like what happened out on the farm, Dad," George answered.

George had an opportunity to let Amos know that General Murphy would have the assailant available for Harry's talents when they got him to the base. Amos and Charlene told them that they had set the date for their wedding.

Amos complained about waiting six months, but told them all, "I'm sure that it will be worth the wait."

The engaged couple looked really happy as they showed Laura the engagement ring.

Laura snuggled up against George and commented, "Isn't that adorable, honey?"

George agreed, "I've never seen either Charlene or Amos look so happy."

The waitress approached with caution as though there was a senator or some important government official at their table, then she recognized George's parents. "Mr. and Mrs. Lee, what in the world is going on here?

Mom Lee said, "Oh, they are watching out for us, making sure nothing happens while we are having lunch, Donna. You know Charlene, don't you? Well, that's her fiancé, Amos. Do you remember George? Well that's his new bride, Laura. Everybody, this is Donna Sparks. She went to school with Charlene."

"I'm pleased to see you all. I think I remember George. He was a couple years ahead of us in school. Congratulations to the newlyweds. Are you ready to order?"

They all ordered and began to talk quietly among themselves secure in the thought that the agents were watching out for their safety. Soon, they began acting like common folk again. Those who had been in the restaurant when the CIA came in stopped watching them so things seemed normal once again.

The meal was quiet, except for the occasional laugh. They were having the time of their lives. Dad, George, and Amos chatted and it seemed like no time until Charlene announced that she had better get back to the office. She stood to leave and Amos also got up and excused himself. He told George that he would be right back as soon as he walked Charlene to her office. They stopped by the register and Amos paid the bill as they left.

As George's family continued their meal and conversation, a man surprised George by tapping him on the shoulder. George jumped, and a CIA agent reached for his pistol.

The man saw what was happening and raised his hands and turned toward the agent and said, "I'm Clyde, I just recognize George and came over to say hello."

George recognized him. "It's okay, Agent Smith, I know him. He's a friend."

The agent secured his weapon and sat back down, but kept his eyes on them.

George stood and gave Clyde a hug. "Clyde Jones, it's been ages. How are you doing? How are your mom and dad?"

Clyde answered, "That's my wife over there sitting with our two sons. Mom and Dad have both passed."

He motioned for her to come over. She got up, but nervously eyed on the agent who nodded that it was okay. She was relieved as she brought their two sons over and

Clyde introduced them, "This is Nancy, my wife, and Miguel and Micah, my two sons."

George shook all their hands and said, "It is so good to meet you guys. Oh, I'm sorry, I almost forgot my manners. This is my wife Laura. We were married about five weeks ago."

Laura stood and hugged each one of them. "It is good to meet you folk. Clyde, you are a lovely family."

They had to rush off so that Clyde could get back to his car sales lot. They all waved as they left.

"Doesn't that make you want to have a child, George?" Laura asked.

Dad joined in, "Yeah Son we need to have some grandchildren before we get too old to play with them, George." He chuckled as he watched George's expression. "All good things will come to pass in good time. Anyway, Charlene and Amos may be the ones to make Mom and me proud grandparents."

The family was ready to leave when George asked his parents if they wanted to do anything while they were in town.

She said, "I need to get a few groceries, George, and there are prescriptions I need to pick up for Dad and me if it wouldn't be too much trouble."

George quietly told an agent to relay the information to Agent Brown who had left to guard the street. He nodded and quickly left. After a short time, he returned and told

George, "Agent Brown said that these stops would be no problem, especially if she was going to get the ingredients for those great donuts she makes."

George whispered something to the agent. He laughed and said, "I don't think that will be a problem."

He walked over to Mrs. Lee and handed her a piece of paper and asked Mrs. Lee, "Would you write down the list of ingredients needed to make those delicious donuts."

She smiled and took the paper and pen and scribbled the ingredients down and then handed the list to the agent. He thanked her and left. Everyone watched as he contacted each agent. Each one grinned and reached into their pockets and pulled a $5 bill. He continued until each agent sitting in the restaurant was contacted and then headed out and did the same with all the agents waiting outside. Everyone was happily anticipating the taste of the donuts as they headed back to the Lee farm especially Agent Brown, who just loved them. He had often told Mrs. Lee that her donuts were the best he had ever tasted, and the other agents agreed.

After Amos returned, the Lee family rode in the rental that Amos had borrowed from George. After the shopping was all done and they headed home, George suggested, "How about a pizza for dinner?"

Everyone agreed so the agent riding with them radioed that they were stopping by to get pizzas for dinner this evening. They all were happy to comply, even the agents.

One of them commented, "What an assignment this is."

None of them could remember an assignment where they had eaten such good-tasting treats.

During their stay, Laura even tried to milk a cow. She caused a lot of smiles, but the cow got a little nervous. The calves and kid goats were so cute and playful that Laura later told George that she almost didn't want to leave.

George told her as they watched a pair twin kids climb the wooden gate to their pen, "We can come here on vacation. I know they are cute, but just remember that I was raised in this atmosphere. It's fun watching them, but sometimes, they really require a lot of work and special care for these little cuties."

Laura said, "Maybe, if the Lord wills and we survive that long, and of course, if God wills it, we will survive to do it."

With the relaxed atmosphere and the increased alertness of the CIA, things remained quiet and pleasurable during the rest of their visit with the Lee family.

CIA vehicles led the convoy to the airport; Amos rode with Charlene in the second vehicle; in the third vehicle was George's parents, Laura, and him; while another CIA vehicle brought up the rear.

On the way, Mom told them, "Dad and I are going to open a donut shop in town. We are going to name it PS Lee's Donut Shop. A couple of the CIA fellows suggested that we should do it and promised to help. They said that they had to hang around us anyway, so they might as well lend a helping hand. I promised them free donuts as payment."

Laura got excited. "Are you sure that your health will allow you handle that?"

"Well, we will make sure it's okay, but I don't think it will be much different than fixing all those donuts for all the agents. After we know if it's going to fly, we can hire someone and Charlene said that she would help with the paperwork and deal with the taxes, at least until the wedding."

Amos had decided to stay at the Lee's farm a bit longer. He could help with the shop, at least until they were married.

It was impossible not to notice that there was something unusual going on upon their arrival at the terminal. Agents entered the building and checked it out before the Lees entered. A couple agents watched over them until they entered then they remained behind to guard the vehicles.

The CIA checked the passenger list, then went aboard the plane, but found no threat. Just before George and Laura entered the ramp to board the plane, all the CIA came to him one by one to express their gratitude and wish Laura and him the best. George gave Charlene a hug and congratulated her for her engagement. He gave Dad and Mom a hug and told them that he loved them and wished them great success with the donut shop. They were the last ones to board the plane and were excited that they were finally going to see their home at the new base.

They waved back at their parents, Charlene, and Amos as the plane was towed away from the terminal. As they waved, George wondered when he would see his friend again, but knew if danger was near, he could count on him being there.

As the plane's nose lifted and the tail dipped, Laura looked over at George and sighed, "Since we've been married, there has been one exciting event after the other. I wonder what new adventure awaits us."